Until Lily

Sherry Boas

To Natalie,
May the Lord bless
all your beautiful
endeavors.

Caritas Press

Until Lily

Sherry Boas

Cover and book design: Sherry Boas

First Edition, 2011

10 9 8 7 6 5 4 3 2 1

ISBN: 978-0-9833866-0-5

Published by Caritas Press, Phoenix, Arizona

For reorders and other inspirational materials visit our website at LilyTrilogy.com

For my TT, who is responsible for nine gray hairs and an uncountable number of smiles. And for her birth mother, whose valiant sacrifice made all of the joy possible.

Until Lily is the first in a trilogy available from Caritas Press.

Until Lily
Wherever Lily Goes
Life Entwined with Lily's

"The Lily Trilogy is a heartwarming look at life through the lens of "pure love." Lily touches your soul in an inspiring way that only one so close to God truly can." -- Tom Peterson, President and Founder, Virtue Media and Catholics Come Home

"As a mother and writer, I enjoyed this book immensely. It's impossible not to become attached to Lily or to sympathize with Bev. Lily's joyful spirit and innocence, and her effect on everyone she meets, speaks so powerfully to the great gift of children with Down Syndrome. And Bev's honest, at times painful, confessions make all of us reconsider our motives and prejudices. "A terrific blend of humor and heart-wrenching tenderness, *Until Lily* shows the goodness that is possible in every human being, and the potential for self-gift that only those who love deeply and sincerely can know. I laughed, I cried and asked myself more than once if I have cherished the true dignity of each person in my own life the way characters in this book do. *Until Lily* is a recommended read for anyone who has ever wondered at the loving purpose of every single person in God's creation." -- Mary Moore, Author, *Rocking the Cradle Catholic: Raising Little Saints in a Lukewarm Culture.*

"Now, more than ever, the world needs to hear the messages embedded in these books, which so beautifully, candidly and, at times, humorously, capture the incredible sacrifices and unmatched rewards of parenthood. This is a story, not just for those with special needs children, but for all parents who struggle in one way or another. And isn't that pretty much all parents?" -- Father Doug Lorig, creator of *A Spirituality of Parenting* video series

"I could not put these books down! Ms. Boas captures the raw emotion and secret thoughts of the human heart and pours them out into novels which will make people think, question, and no doubt view the sanctity of every life with more value. The depth of the characters and the very real situations they encounter draw the reader into story lines that touch on every point of human life – from conception to death – with humor, tenderness and, above all, a realness sure to penetrate anyone lucky enough to find these gems." – Kristina L. Forbes, mother of seven and former Director of Counselor Training, Aid to Women Center

Visit www.lilytrilogy.com

Contents

1

BEDSIDE VEGETABLES

I keep my hair long for one reason only. Lily likes to brush it. But today it was so muggy, I was half considering a trip down the hall to the beauty shop. I can't stand my hair sticking to my neck, and I can't put it up, my arms hurt so bad. If it weren't for Lily, I would have probably succumbed to the Primp and Pamper long ago. There's something strange about that place, though. Three hours after a woman enters, she emerges arm-in-arm with the hair dresser, who parades her around the nursing home as if she were unveiling an original piece of commissioned art. The hair sculpture is met with polite acclaim from residents and staff, but it is chiefly the same as the last client's and will be, you can bet, not much different from the next. How could curlers and a backcomb yield such uniform results? Makes you wonder if there isn't some equivalent to a Jell-O mold for hair. There's an age at which people expect you to command a certain amount of predictability -- if not obedience -- from your hair. Though I've long since passed that age, it's been three decades since I had a real hair cut. Twice a year, I split my hair down the middle, bring it in front of me and trim the ends back up to my hip bones. I developed this method years ago, as a way of ensuring I never cut too much off. When Lily was little, she liked to play car wash as I tipped my head down and let her run through my hair. She would cackle and rake at her cheeks as if to rid her face of a soapy residue. A bouffant would have zapped a certain measure of joy from that child's life.

The lobby of the Manor House nursing home is decorated with stars-and-stripes buntings -- the plastic kind you get from MacFrugal's -- hung from wall-mounted light fixtures resembling upside-down tulips. Red, white and blue streamers are draped too close to the foam ceiling to be truly festive. Couldn't they have worked a few more feet of crepe paper into the budget? After all, they're getting good mileage out of the patriotic theme. They put it up for Flag Day and leave it through the Fourth of July. The staff here tells Lily it's for her birthday. She was born on June 14, 2011, which makes her 34 this year.

"It's close to 5 o'clock, Bev," Agnes says. "Why don't you call her?" Agnes always waits in the lobby with me for Lily to come. She calls her my angel. She honestly believes in such things.

"We'll give her a few more minutes," I say. I know Agnes is making the same calculations I am. What would delay Lily by 22 minutes?

Agnes is my best friend. She came just before I did, almost three years ago now. Since we were both new, we found common ground right away in a two-part question: How in the Sam Hill did we end up in this place and how long until they wheel us out of here under a white sheet?

Aside from the seasonal decorations, the place always looks the same, like a Museum for the Slowly Dying. Same poor souls parked in the same spots. Over in the far corner is Buddy. He's the youngest one here -- probably in his early 40's. He sits in his wheelchair and glares. I've seen neighborhood children come to visit here, handing out candy or homemade cookies or St. Patrick's Day shamrocks cut out of construction paper and generously doused with green glitter. Buddy will reach out and take what ever the child has to offer and never say a word or relent from his scowl. They assume he can't talk, and it's a good thing he doesn't, because I've heard what comes out of his mouth when he does, and it's not suitable for small children trying to be the bright spot in someone's day. Not even the meanest nurses here deserve that level of verbal abuse. Well, maybe one of them does. There is a male nurse who will shake Buddy's bed in the middle of the night just to hear him spout profanities.

I reach for my walker. "I'm going to get my cell phone," I say to Agnes. Whenever Lily is late, which isn't very often, I put off calling her because she forgets to carry her cell half the time anyway. If I call and she doesn't answer, we just end up worrying all the harder.

"I'll wait here for her," Agnes says. She has taken ownership of my daily visitor. She has none of her own.

A pain shoots from my hip down my leg like an electrical current as I pull myself up. If people rusted, I'd be creaking like an old back-porch glider. I never thought I would get this old or that it would hurt this much. The sterile linoleum hallway lined by handrails, dotted with fake wood doors every five feet, might as well be the route for the Tour de France. Every time I make this journey I wish Lily was here. She walks backwards in front of me, letting my hands press into hers to keep me from falling forward. The walker is OK, but it doesn't have the sixth sense that Lily does about when to ease up on the pressure against my palms, or when to tighten the grip on my trembling hands. Every time she walks me, I think about when she was little. I had to pull her along everywhere, her arm fully stretched, her hand trapped in mine. By the end of the day, my biceps would ache from the strain of keeping her on my schedule.

"Come on, keep up," I'd say looking back over my shoulder to find her looking back over hers at some blade of grass growing up through a crack in the sidewalk. She'd heed my urging and walk a little faster for five or ten paces, but then something would catch her attention again. I always wondered why she was never interested in anything in front of her, only things she had already passed -- the wagging tail of a Chihuahua, her reflection in a store window, the shiny tab from a soda can. Even with no distractions, the best she could manage was an apathetic waddle. I think about this often when she's standing in for my walker

3

and I feel her fleshy hands in mine. Her head is down, watching my feet as if they were cherished children. She looks into my eyes every few steps and flashes me a smile. She has all day to walk me twenty feet. Not because she has nowhere else to go, but because loving me is both journey and destination. Back when I was the able-bodied one, my destination was always the grocery store or the park or the school. Why couldn't she ever have been my destination? She was more like a nail in my tire. I wish her hand could be little in mine again.

There are a number of things I'd like to do over. Out of the three kids, I always gave Lily the smallest piece or the broken one or the color no one else wanted. I justified it by saying she didn't care, because most of the time, she seemed not to notice. But I think maybe deep down I resented her for changing my life. Well, I'm not so sure I resented her so much as I did my sister. Every time I'd see Lily fall down or struggle with a button or try to get her point across with a series of grunts and hand motions, the thought would surface, as much as I hated it to. It was my sister's fault, my sister whom I loved dearly, but who betrayed reason and eventually me.

The solo trek down the hallway is over. I've made it to my door without toppling. Monique, my roommate, is sleeping, as she has been for weeks, her mouth a dark cave agape below sharp cheek bones and pointed nose. Her head is tipped back as if she were in a permanent gasp for air. She looks like something from a nightmare you have after eating too many radishes. Her salmon-colored blanket reveals the outline of what looks like the skeleton of a 10-year-old girl.

I shuffle my feet past her to my night stand and open the top drawer to grab my phone. Lily doesn't answer. I sit on the bed watching Monique sleep. If she weren't snoring so loudly, I'd swear she was dead. And I doubt anyone would notice. How could a woman named Monique end up this way? Monique is the name of beautiful girls who have to put their dates in palm pilots to keep them straight. She must have had a handsome, successful husband at one time. He must have bought her fancy clothes and designer fragrances. She must have borne him gorgeous, honor rolled children. But there's been no sight of anyone, except for a younger sister who comes by once a month and talks over her to the nurse about "how much longer."

When visitors come calling at the Manor House -- on holidays, birthdays or odd weekends -- it's always with that far-off look in their eyes. They are serving their time here. They are appeasing their consciences. For mercy's sake, Josie, the receptionist, should just pass out a form at the door with all the excuses necessary to make a quick exit. Just check one:

Have to work.
Have to get Junior to the baseball field.
Have to get to the grocery store. (No milk in the fridge.)
Have to do laundry (Underwear drawer empty.)
Have to mail a package before the post office closes.
Have to nurse the baby.
Have to get to sleep early. (Big day tomorrow.)
Have to let the dog out. (Just got new carpet.)
Have to let the cat in.
Have to meet the plumber. (Junior flushed toy truck.)
Have to get home to spouse. (Wife ovulating.)

I don't mean to brag, but my visitor doesn't need a fast-exit form. They practically have to call a bouncer to get Lily to leave. The nurses have actually learned to give her 15, 10 and 5-minute warnings that visiting hours are coming to an end. She would curl up with me in my bed and stay all night if they would let her. Once she asked the nurses if she could spend the night for her birthday. They explained to her that the important men dressed in suits wouldn't agree to that because she's not a paid resident. So she reached into her purse and pulled out a five-dollar bill. That made them smile. I'm the envy of this whole place to have someone come visit every day. Most residents have children like my Terry and Jimmy. They're not selfish or ungrateful kids. They're just busy. Busy with their children and their jobs. I see them once or twice a year when they fly in to Seattle. Terry is an interior designer in Minneapolis and Jimmy is an engineer in Denver.

My leg begins to tremble and I lift it onto the bed. I stare up at the shelf on the wall opposite my bed where I keep everything that Lily brings me. A cereal box promoting the re-release of *Finding Nemo*, because that's a movie we've watched together for close to thirty years. A bunch of dried wildflowers she picked from a vacant lot on the way here. A take-out menu from a restaurant where she went on a date, because she wished I could have been there. A small chocolate box from a chocolate factory tour where the participants in her day program went for a field trip. A pink teddy bear wearing a green polka dot party hat. A philodendron she bought at the grocery store where she works. A framed picture of Lily in a blue bathing suit and white swim cap, beaming and holding a bronze medal after competing in Special Olympics. A statue of Mary that Lily had blessed by her favorite priest -- Father Julio, I think it was. On the wall under the shelf, I hang all of Lily's pencil drawings. Her style has evolved through the years from typical stick figures and circles forming two-dimensional flowers to a primitive folk art depicting wild, running animals. I can only attribute that to the multitude of Wild Kingdom episodes she used to watch with Jimmy. I think Lily's style is quite irresistible, and I've been trying to get her to consider selling her drawings on e-bay, but she insists on giving them away. I think just about every nurse has received an antelope pursued by a lion, signed in the lower right-hand corner with a heart and a lily.

I hear voices coming closer down the hallway. It's Lily and Agnes. I close my eyes and sigh. They round the door jam, Lily pushing Agnes in her wheelchair.

"I found your angel," Agnes says.

"Hi, Mommy." Lily rushes toward me in a quick waddle and gives me a hug and a kiss on the cheek and lays her head on my chest.

"Hi, baby," I say, laying my shaking arms over her. "I tried to call you. Did you forget your cell phone?"

"I sawry," she says, looking into my eyes. "I forgot. I lef- the can of corn on my night stand, jus- like Miss Jean say. Because I wanta member something. To get my phone off the charger and put it in my purse. But I woke up and saw the corn and can- member why I put the corn there. It din' work, did it?" She lets out a small giggle. A full-blown belly laugh follows.

I chuckle. "I guess not, Lily."

Most of us would write ourselves a note, but since writing has always been a struggle for Lily, her therapist suggested other ways. On mornings when you have to put the trash out, for instance, you put a can of vegetables on your night stand. As soon as you wake up, you see the can and it reminds you you're supposed to do something out of the ordinary that day. It's similar to the string around the finger trick, but it works better, because you can eventually grow accustomed to the string and begin to ignore it. It's hard to ignore vegetables in the bedroom.

"Maybe try peas next time," I tell Lily.

"No," she says smirking. "I don' like peas."

Lily never would eat anything green. When the kids were little, I used to make them tri-color pasta. All three colors tasted exactly the same, but Lily would eat the orange and yellow and leave the green on her plate. If I could have convinced her it was pasta, it would have been gone in three seconds, but I never could. She would have lived completely on starch and cheese if I would have let her. Well, buttered starch. I can't tell you how many tantrums were thrown over butter. I learned to let the toast cool to room temperature before buttering it because if the butter melted and she couldn't see it any more, the whole household paid. Butter had to be in big closely-spaced clumps. Because she was a little on the chubby side and has a small hole in her heart, I was always walking a fine line, trying to get away with as little butter as possible without triggering a meltdown.

"Why are you late, Honey?" I ask.

"Well, work all done, I buy someting, I miss the bus." She makes a mock sad face.

"What did you buy?"

"No, I can' tell you," she smiles wide. "It's a surprise. For you birtday."

"My birthday is four months away," I say.

"It's a long surprise," she says grinning. "Something I give you from my heart."

That's Lily. Everything happens from her heart.

"I bring something for you, too, Agnes," she says, bounding to the doorway where Agnes' chair is parked. Lily gives her a hug.

"Oh, thank you, Angel," Agnes says kissing her on the forehead. "I just love you."

"I love you too, Agnes," Lily says. On her way back to me, she looks at poor Monique. "Should I get someting for her too?"

"If you'd like," I say.

"OK. I will," she says. "Mommy, can I comb your hair?"

"Sure. Can you put it up for me, Honey?"

Agnes excuses herself to go wash up for dinner. Lily combs hair like a neurosurgeon operates, as if tangles were malignant and her efforts could save a life. I never have had that kind of patience for hair. Lily could attest to that if she ever remembered a person's past transgressions, which she doesn't. She always had an extremely high threshold for pain. When she was little, she would have blood drawn and never flinch. She'd get a shot and smile at the nurse for putting a Scooby-Doo Band-aid on the injection site. But I would pick up a hairbrush and she'd burst into a red-faced cry, take off running and hurl a variety of household objects in my path. When she'd run out of escape route, she'd wedge her head between the couch cushions and scream.

I remember my uncle, who was a police officer, talking about a phenomenon in law enforcement that often explains the prevalence of police brutality. A perpetrator leads officers on such an intense chase that by the time they catch him, the cops' adrenalin is pumped so high, they can't stop themselves from beating the guy senseless, even after he's splayed out on the ground in a paralyzed surrender.

It was sort of like that at hair-brushing time in our house. By the time I caught Lily, I no longer had the capacity for kind and gentle, patient coaxing. My heart would be pounding so hard, I thought my chest would explode. Maybe my head too. A gardener would probably go easier on the hedges than I did on poor Lily's head. But this brushing thing had turned into a match of wills. If there was a tangle left in her hair after I got through with her, it would have meant that she had won, and I had never been a gracious loser. If I had to put Lily into a half-nelson in order to tie the pretty pink ribbon in her beautiful hair, so be it.

"Almos-' done, Mommy," Lily says. "I o-ly have one part lef-. Then do you wanna go ou-side?"

"Oh, I'm so tired today, baby," I say, trying to pin my shaking thumb between my two fingers, so I can remove a hang nail. "Maybe we can try tomorrow."

"But it so pretty ou-side," she pleads. "I get the chair."

"Why is it pretty?"

"Nice and warm. And the flowers," she says, erupting into a smile. "Make my heart happy. I wanna pick some for you."

"Well, we can't pick those, you know," I say, just in case she needs reminding. "Someone planted them."

"I know. I know." Lily's hands are damp and rubbery on my hairline as she meticulously gathers all the stray hairs off my face. "Thish ish going to be pretty pony tail." She holds the elastic band in her teeth as she speaks. As if it isn't already hard enough to understand her. "Can I go ask for the wheelchair? Or you walk?"

"I can't walk today, Lily," I say. "Get the chair, and I'll sit on my crazy hands." There are times when sitting on them to keep them still is my only relief. There are other times when sitting on them hurts too much.

Lily's smile grows wide at the thought of pushing me around the grounds. She's already in the hallway when she remembers to poke her head back through the doorway and say, "I be righ- back." You typically only see that kind of enthusiasm when you tell a kid she's going to Disney Land. For Lily, Disney-caliber elation occurs seven or eight times a day. I wonder what it would be like to feel life to that depth. What if that's the way we're all supposed to be made and it's the rest of us with the disability? Not so very long ago, I would have dismissed that thought as ridiculous. Thirty five years ago, I would have considered it insane.

****

It was New Year's Eve 2010. Jack and I had just turned on the TV to watch the ball drop on Times Square, as we had done all 15 years of our marriage, except for the time when Jack rented a Lincoln town car and drove me to the Crowne Plaza Hotel. He had sold so many insurance policies that year that his boss booked him a room on the 29th floor, and we watched the Space Needle's midnight fireworks display from our bed while drinking Champaign on 1,000 thread-count sateen. We had a bit too much to do that night to turn on the TV. In 2010, however, we were sitting on separate recliners, wearing shearling slippers, drinking Heineken beers, eating cold cuts and watching strangers make fools of themselves on national television. In some respects, it was almost as fun as the Crowne Plaza, and we both knew that sometime before 12:15, we would pop down our foot rests, walk down the hall, shed our flannel and slip into bed together to make predictably satisfying love. The telephone rang just as I was taking the first bite out of a Salami and Provolone sandwich. FOX had gone to a Coca-Cola commercial and Jack had gone to the bathroom.

It was Jen, my little sister, calling to wish us Happy New Year and tell us she's pregnant.

"What?"

"Uh-huh," she said. "You heard me."

"Well, congratulations." I was a little unsure what to say to a single, 39-year-old pregnant woman. I thought maybe congratulations weren't so crazy considering she had adopted two other children.

"It's not good, Bev," she said.

"What do you mean not good?"

"The baby has Down Syndrome."

"Oh, I'm sorry Jenny girl," I said. "You must be devastated."

A large quantity of exhaled air whistled through the telephone line. "I just really don't know how I'm going to manage it all. I mean it's already hard enough."

Jen's adopted children were a handful. They didn't have visible disabilities, but they had come from rough beginnings.

"It'll be OK, Jen," I said. "I'll fly out and take care of Terry and Jimmy. I can get away from the store for a few days."

"I'm not really worried about delivery day, Bev," Jen said. "I'm worried about the next 50 years."

"Oh." I know this was the longest silence that had ever passed between us. But I didn't know how to clarify what I thought I was hearing. Finally I just had to put it out there. "You're going to have the baby."

"Well, yeah." As if this was a no-brainer.

"You know, most people wouldn't, Jen," I said. "The baby is not right."

"Bev, you know we weren't raised like that." Here we go with the religion stuff. We weren't exactly raised to conceive while unmarried either.

"How far along are you?" I asked. I wondered how much time I had to try to change her mind.

"Fourteen weeks."

As soon as I got off the phone, I went on-line and learned that at fourteen weeks, the fetus is only three inches long and weighs only an ounce. What exactly was my sister trying to save? I also found in my research that 90 percent of Down Syndrome fetuses are aborted. Armed with this enlightening knowledge, I crafted all my subsequent e-mails for the next several weeks to focus on the humanity of the choice to terminate. All the medical problems, suffering the child would endure, struggling through life's simplest tasks, rejection, low self esteem, isolation, and the straight-out sadness at being different. I had formulated a theory, which I only hinted at, that the reason Jen was going through with this was not for the sake of the child, but because she herself wanted so badly to be pregnant. Hers was a kind of selfishness, veiled in faux morality.

When we were little kids, Jen always used to pretend to be pregnant. We saw a neighbor of ours in like her eighth month, and our mother explained to us that there was a baby growing inside her tummy, and Jen just thought that was the most intriguing thing. She'd get one of Dad's big T-shirts and put it on and stuff a pillow under it and look at herself in the mirror sideways, then front ways, then sideways again. Whenever we'd play house, she'd be the mom with one baby and one on the way. I'm sure she studied Mrs. Crenshaw next door to see how she walked and sat and got up. She did everything just like her. Me, I was never interested in being pregnant or even the Mom. I always wanted to be the teenage babysitter, who talked on the phone to her boyfriend while watching the latest videos on MTV.

****

Lily has walked me out to the courtyard. We sit in the shade under the trellis of grapevines, so thick after 22 years since the Manor House opened, that the birds nest there. Lily deals the cards, while my hands fumble to collect them into a pile. Lily fixes hers into a tidy deck and then reaches for mine, to save me the frustration. My long slender fingers, not so long ago able and agile, now are gawky and warped like the witch's from the Wizard of Oz. Lily's fingers are still stubby -- just a larger version of the ones she must have been born with. But I marvel at how well they work. Fifteen years of occupational therapy did its service.

"You first, Mommy," Lily says placing her hand on top of her deck. When playing War, two players can technically go at the same time, but Lily doesn't like to play that way. She likes to prolong the suspense by having the other player put a card down first. She gets a sheepish grin on her face before she reveals her card, as if there were some sort of strategy to the game, which requires only that you, by luck of the draw, play the highest card in order to capture your opponent's.

A seven and a Jack.

"Hu-ha!" Lily shouts, swooping the two cards toward her. "I win that one."

I had learned, with shaking hands, how to flick the cards onto the table so they would land face side up.

Three, nine.

"I win again!" Lily says.

Four, five.

She gathers the cards in like a miser, biting her bottom lip into an endearing grin. Then she looks into my face. "Don- worry, Mommy. You can still win."

"Who shuffled these cards, anyway?" I ask feigning indignation.

Six, ace.

"Here, you have this one," she says, pushing the cards toward me.

"No, remember Ace is high." My hands tremble the cards in Lily's direction.

"No, it's OK, Mommy." She pushes the cards back toward me. "You don't have any."

"Hey, I don't want any pity points," I tell her. "My luck just hasn't kicked in yet. I'm going to kick your butt."

Lily bursts into a giggle. Any sentence with the word "butt" gets an automatic laugh. When we were teaching Lily her alphabet, the kids and I used to play this game where we would sit in a circle and toss a ball to each other. The person who caught the ball would have to come up with a word that started with the next letter in the alphabet. Terry and Jimmy would always jockey for the position that would make them the second one to go, so they could say "B" is for butt. Everyone would roll around laughing, no matter how many times we played the game. It never got old. As for myself, I only rarely used the word. I reserved it for times when someone was seriously upset or injured. I wonder if Terry and Jimmy ever use it for comedy relief with their kids.

"Your turn, Mommy." Lily says.

"Oh, I'm sorry, Lil." I watch my first two fingers fumble with the top card of my deck until my thumb decides to cooperate.

Queen, two.

"Ha! Told ya!" I spank my hands down on the cards that had won me a round.

"Yay, you got one," Lily cheers.

Lily doesn't like to lose, but she doesn't like to win, either. That's something I learned quite a few years ago when she competed in the Special Olympics. Lily was really a good swimmer -- as good, if not better, than many people without disabilities. She was the favorite going into the race, but people underestimated her generosity. Whenever she'd get too far ahead of the other swimmers, she'd slow down and wait for them. You don't win any gold medals that way, but you do win hearts. People crowded around to congratulate her after the race for a true victory -- one of solidarity with her fellow athletes.

"Can we play this again tomorrow?" Lily asks, laying her head on the table to get a better look at the height of the stack of cards she has won.

"Sure," I say.

"Can we play every day?"

"Maybe."

"Forever and ever? I love this game. It my favorite."

"You should teach your friends to play it, so you will always have someone to play with."

"Oh, no. I only play with you." She drums her first and second fingers on her stack of cards in an off-beat rhythm. "No one can do it. Jus' you. I won- play if you won- play. I won- play anything."

"What about a boyfriend? Would you play War with a boy- friend?"

Lily stops drumming and flashes a bashful smile. "Oh, no. I don- have one of those."

"But you may someday."

"And we can get marry?"

"Sure."

"And have seven babies."

"Wow. That's a lot of babies."

"An- he be the Daddy and I be the Mommy."

"Uh-huh."

"I love daddies."

"I know."

"I wanna see my Daddy. Where my Daddy?"

"You mean Jack? He's in Heaven, remember?"

"No, the Daddy with the puppy. An- where the puppy?"

"The puppy?"

"I saw a picture long time ago. There was me and a puppy. The Daddy bring the puppy."

I don't have the heart to tell Lily that her mother instructed me thirty years ago never to contact Lily's birth father, for rea- sons that have remained mysterious and, to me, somewhat sad. I would love for Lily to have the Daddy she has always wanted. I have been so often tempted to betray my promise to my sister and track Lily's father down. Now, with my failing health, a be- trayal makes more sense than ever. Lily needs someplace to deposit all that unbounded love. Someplace besides me.

2

OPERATIC PIG

When Lily was born in June 2011, Jen never called to tell me. The first time I heard from her was that Christmas. I e-mailed her a Season's Greetings and she e-mailed me back a nativity e-card and pictures of the kids. For several years after that, we called each other on holidays and she e-mailed pictures of the kids on their birthdays. All correspondence was cordial. Jen had always built me and Jack up in the minds of the children as something special. We always tried to live up to that. Since our parents had passed away and there was no other family, it was up to Jack and me to spoil them. It wasn't difficult. Nice children's books were always coming into the used book store I owned, and I would wrap them up and Fed-Ex them, many times on no special occasion. I'd always include in the parcel a little something for the kids to play with and a treat to eat. Peanut M & M's were Jimmy and Terry's favorites and they were hardy during shipping.

In the spring of 2015, Jen invited us out to Burbank for a visit. When she picked us up at the airport, I almost walked right past her. She had gotten so thin, and the children were all so big. I couldn't believe so many years had passed, and I was the only one who hadn't changed. Lily, a plump four-year-old, was the first to give me a hug. She had the classic Down's features -- a flat-bridged nose and small eyes slanted upward with fleshy folds of skins on the inner corners. I had always thought all people with Down Syndrome looked alike, but I was struck by how much Lily looked like Jen with her round cheeks and pointed chin. She had shiny dark hair fashioned into pigtails that reminded me of Jen's kindergarten picture, which Mom had always kept on the mantle, along with my second-grade portrait. When I say always, I mean always. The realtor who did the walk-through at the house after Mom and Dad died told us we had to take the photos down to get maximum dollar. Apparently, prospective home buyers only want to envision their own family on the mantle, and pictures of someone else's children distract them from the fantasies you want them to have about how dreamy it would be like to live in your house.

As we waited for our baggage, I watched Lily try to befriend an elderly man filling out a form, which from the look on his face, must have been a missing luggage report. She smiled at him and reached her hand toward his. He seemed to resent that she had barged into his entitled misery with her irresistible charms, but he finally conceded to her hand in his and managed a slight smile. You could no more avoid the radiance of that child's face than you could stand blinking up at the sun and forbid its rays to warm you.

Everyone fought over who would sit next to Jack on the way to Jen's house. We worked it out so Jack would sit in the middle of Terry and Jimmy in the back seat of the mini-van. Lily got the consolation prize. She got to sit by me in the middle row. She kept looking over at me, smiling and giving me a breathy "hi," every couple of miles. Meanwhile, Jimmy and Terry competed for airtime as Jack asked them questions. Favorite sport, favorite subject in school, favorite TV show, favorite movie. Jen sat in the front seat by herself, driving. She only spoke to interject an occasional "yeah," or "uh-huh," when the kids would say, "remember that, Mom?" I leaned forward a bit and noticed Jen's crow's feet and sagging jaw-line. I thought her skin hung quite loose for a woman of 44. She'd been running too hard.

"So, Jen," I said. "How's work? What have you been writing lately?"

"Oh, it's fine. I've been taking some time off." She glanced in the rearview mirror. "But I just found out I won a press award for a story I wrote last year."

"Really? For what?" I asked.

"A feature on a woman whose husband was shot on their wedding anniversary."

"Wow," I said. "So you're still covering cops?"

"No. I moved to features a few months ago. It is just a lot more manageable."

"Congratulations on your award, Jen," Jack said from the back seat.

"You lose!" said Jimmy, shoving Jack playfully.

There had been a lull in the conversation back there since Jack suggested playing the "quiet game" following Jimmy's and Terry's argument about whether terradactiles picked the flesh off of carcasses and ate it.

"Did the award come with any money?" I asked Jen.

"A whopping $100 and a wall plaque."

"Let's play again," Jimmy said. "This time, whoever wins gets 100 bucks."

"No, I don't want to play," said Terry.

"And how's the store?" Jen asked.

"It's still there," I said. "Nothing new to report." There was never anything new in the used-book business. "So, when am I going to be stocking my shelves with your best-selling novel?"

I'd always admired Jen's writing genius. Maybe even envied it. She was a true wordsmith. Me, I just knew good writing when I saw it. But Jen had an innate gift, for sure. Mom used to say she'd find me with my nose in a book all the time and Jen with a pencil in her hand. She started writing a novel when she was eight, just for fun. It was a chapter book about her and our dog, Dusty, catching a robber while house sitting for neighbors. Jen and I found it in the attic after Mom passed away. We were both surprised how good the writing was. I always wondered how she knew how to write, since she hardly ever read. She had very poor eyesight and double vision and the words just wouldn't sit still on the page. She told me when we were kids how she used to fake it in class during silent reading assignments by watching when the student next to her turned the page and then turning hers too. And she used to cheat on book reports by just reading the back cover and the first and last chapters. She never read a text book all through high school. She said that very rarely -- if ever -- did something that wasn't spoken of in class show up on a test, and thus she managed straight A's. It was not until she reached college that she had to start reading. The first semester she decided not to bother purchasing the textbooks and nearly flunked a geography class. The next seven semesters the student book store got all her money and she pulled a 4.0 every time. It required quite a time investment on her part because she was -- and still is -- a painfully slow reader. I've heard her say she can write faster than she can read, which might not be much of an exaggeration, because I've seen the quantity of work she produces on deadline in a day.

"Uncle Jack, can you and Aunt Bev take us to see *Wander-loo*?" Jimmy asked. We were sitting at a stoplight in front of a 16-theater AMC. "I really want to see it."

"It's PG-13, Jimmy," Terry said, rolling her eyes.

"So?" he countered. "Mom let us see Indiana Jones."

"That's not PG-13, genius," Terry said contemptuously.

"Yes, it is."

"No, it's not."

"It's PG," Terry shouted.

"Drop it, you two," Jen said, raising her eyebrows in the rear-view mirror. Then her face softened. "And how's your job, Jack?"

"Not nearly as exciting as yours, I'm afraid," Jack said.

"Oh, being a reporter isn't all that exciting either," Jen said.

"No, I was talking about your other job," Jack said, grinning, pointing his nose at Jimmy, then Terry.

"Oh, yes, that one's exciting," Jen said, without a tinge of irony.

Jen and the kids showed us to Terry and Lily's room, where we would be staying for the week. The double bed was dressed in lime-green and shared by two girls who clearly loved horses, dogs and small people. On the floor was a large pile of Polly Pockets and accessories that had just been dumped out of a canvas cube. The white shelves were cluttered with My Little Ponies, Littlest Pet shop bobbing-head animals and Equestrian books. Amidst the half-dozen horse posters, a crucifix and a picture of the Virgin Mary, I could somehow make out that the wall was baby blue.

"Honey, I asked you to make sure your room was clean," Jen complained to Terry.

"I did," Terry answered with a furrowed brow. "Lily made that mess."

"It looks wonderful in here, girls," I said. "Thanks for lending us your room. But where are you going to sleep?"

"With Mom."

"Oh, Jen," I said. "I don't want to put you out like that."

"No, no," she said. "I enjoy sleeping with my girls. We're going to have a slumber party, right girls?"

"Um-hmmm," Terry said, smiling. Lily just looked at Jen, expressionless.

"No fair," said Jimmy. "I don't get to sleep with anyone."

"You can sleep with us too," Jen said.

"Mom, it's going to be too crowded," Terry whined.

"Oh, good grief, Terry," Jen said. "It's a king-sized bed."

"And who are these little people?" I stooped down and picked up a Polly with yellow hair and hot-pink lipstick and held it out toward Lily.

She took it from me and smiled slightly.

"What's her name?" I asked.

"Lil," she said.

"Oh, her name's Lily too," I confirmed.

"Yeah," she said.

"Well, where are all the cool boy's toys, Jimmy," Jack said.

"Oh, come on, Uncle Jack," Jimmy said. "See my room."

The boys went to the room next door.

"I can see you still like horses, Terry," I said.

She nodded and smiled.

Jen put an arm around her. "She has always loved horses. One time, when she was just little, maybe about 4 or 5, we were driving by a pasture and I glanced back at her and she was staring out the window with these big tears in her eyes, and she said to me, 'Mom, I have horses in my soul.'"

"I want to live out in the country some day and have my own horse," Terry said. "Mom wants goats."

"Oh, you're going to be a goatherd someday, Jen?" I said, nudging her arm with my elbow. "I never knew you had such high aspirations."

"Just craving the simple life," she said, squeezing Terry in a little closer.

The following night, after the kids went to bed, Jen set Jack up in the family room with the cable television remote and a bottle of beer. Then she brewed a pot of tea and told me she needed to talk to me. Upon taking the first sip, she blurted out three words that would eventually save my life.

"Bev, I'm dying."

"What do you mean, you're dying?"

"I have cancer."

From her lips, to my stomach. The words punched me hard. "Cancer? What kind of cancer?"

"Metastatic Melanoma," she said.

"What is that?" I asked, appalled.

"Skin cancer that has spread," she said. "To the other organs."

Her eyes wandered around on my face and she bit her bottom lip, waiting for a response. I couldn't respond because I didn't believe her. Well, that's not true. People don't lie or joke about this kind of thing. It's not that I didn't believe *her*. I didn't believe *it*. Whatever it was that was trying to create this reality -- I didn't believe it.

"Not breast cancer?" I finally said. That was the first clue that this can't be true. Mom had died of breast cancer, not skin cancer. Jen and I were at risk for breast cancer. That's what we would die of, if one of us was dying.

"No, Bev. Not breast cancer."

"Well, what do you mean you're dying? There's no treatment?" See, that was another thing. People you know don't just say they're dying and then die. That's what soap characters do. Real people have some sort of hope through medication or surgery.

"No, Bev. It's spread. I don't have long."

"How long?"

"Three months, maybe six." There you go. What a ridiculous notion. How can a disease take a perfectly healthy person that quickly? Although she did look skinny and her color was not right. I noticed it when she took her makeup off the night before. She had a gray tint to her skin.

"There's got to be some sort of treatment they can try," I said. "Experimental drugs. Alternative medicine. Something."

"No, there's nothing. The cancer has spread to my lungs and brain. That's pretty much a death sentence."

"Pretty much?"

"Is."

"How long have you known?"

She stretched her torso out and took a deep breath. "I went in a couple of months ago for a swollen lymph node. In my groin."

I heard myself draw a long breath, but it didn't come out. I could feel my heart beating against the walls of my chest like the space inside me had suddenly grown too small. What was I going to do without my only sister? My only remaining family member? I would be without any remnant from my childhood.

And then, something in my brain flipped a switch, and the telephoto lens that had been documenting my small world crashing in on me, zoomed out to a wider angle. There in that colorless frame, muted by the shadow of grief, stood the children.

I heard myself let out a small gasp. "Do the children know?"

"They know I've been sick. They don't know the latest prognosis. I'm waiting for our pastor to return from a pilgrimage to the holy land so he can be here when I tell them. He's the one who baptized all of them and gave Terry her First Communion. I figure he'll be able to answer their questions better than anyone else I know. I wish Mom and Dad were still alive. I know Mom would know what to say."

Our eyes couldn't contain the tears any longer. I reached across the table and grabbed her hand.

"I've been so scared to tell them." She forced the thin words through a crackling throat. "I'm especially worried about Jimmy. He's been so afraid of me dying. Even when there was no reason, he would tell me he's afraid. I'd always promised him I wouldn't die. I hope he doesn't hold it against me." She began to sob and I held her head tight against my chest. "I don't want to leave them. I would do anything to stay with them."

"They'll understand that," I whispered. "They'll know this is all out of your control."

"I don't know what I can tell them to make this not seem like the nightmare that it is."

"They just have to be assured that they will be taken care of."

I reached for a napkin and gave it to Jen for her eyes. Then I took one for myself. The picture in my head showed only the three children, stunned with sorrow. There was no one else in the frame.

"Who *is* going to take care of them?" I asked.

Jack and I never had kids and it never bothered us. We grew accustomed to our carefree ways and never considered adopting. We didn't even get a dog because we didn't want to be tied down. Jen, on the other hand, was so afraid she'd never find a man and have a family, that at the age of 35, she stood in front of a Superior Court judge and gave her life to two complete strangers, aged 1 and 2.

23

I know Jack and I were not ideal, not by a long shot. But as the only surviving relative under the age of 82, Jen had no choice. I had to be honest right out front and tell Jen we were not able to care for her children. We were not set up to handle Down Syndrome. Heck, we weren't set up to handle a child of any sort. Anyone who could do the math could figure that out. I was 49 and Jack was 53.

"Don't worry about your age," Jen said. "At least you won't be going through menopause when the kids are going through puberty." She was apparently trying to lighten the conversation, but I felt like my throat would burst. "Can you imagine how much fur would fly with that amount of hormonal imbalance going on?"

Because she was older than most mothers, she told me, she knew she would be going through menopause before her kids left the house. She said she had prayed in advance that she wouldn't get moody and take it out on her children. She told God "give me hot flashes, a thick waist line, incontinence and insomnia, but don't let me turn into a monster to live with." So it didn't surprise her, when early menopause hit, that she would awake every night on wet sheets with her drenched night gown sticking to her like a newly applied layer of paper mache. Never, she said, did she experience a moment of irritability attributed to hormonal changes.

I never even asked Jack what he thought about Jen's proposal because I knew already what I thought.

"We need to make sure to do everything we can for those kids," Jack told me as he held me in bed that night. "Tell Jen. We'll do everything we can."

Jack was a good man that way. He couldn't stand to see anyone suffer.

I had a long cry in the dark until Jack's chest hairs were soaked.

"Bev," he whispered into my hair. "If you're saying no to Jen because of me, don't say no."

"It's not because of you, Jack," I said. "It's because of me."

I tried not to feel guilty about the decision not to take on the kids. It was, after all, Jen's choices that had led to this point, not ours. I didn't want to live the life she had set up. Jen was a bit hurt, I think, but she understood me. I think she knew that she and I were two different people. She was an extremely accepting person and she was able to treat my self-centeredness as if it were my -- for lack of a better word -- handicap. It's like science fiction writer Robert Heinlein once said, "Never try to teach a pig to sing. It wastes your time and annoys the pig." I think Jen knew she might as well have asked a pig to learn opera. I don't think she cared too much about annoying the pig, but she certainly could not afford to waste any time.

Jack and I flew home three days later with the understanding that we would be back within the next few months to say good-bye. In the meantime, we would do all we could to help sort out the children's future. As the cancer made her weaker and the day of her passing closer, Jen began to call and pressure me into taking the kids.

"Oh, Jen, Honey, I thought we had this worked out," I told her.

"Bev, you know I wouldn't ask this of you if there were any other way," she said. "I just don't know what else I can do. My kids are everything to me. I don't like to beg, but I will for my children. I have been reduced to nothing, Bev. I have nothing to offer and only the world to ask of you. So I'm asking. I'm begging, actually. What else can I ..." If the pent up tears hadn't choked off the sentence, I would have had more time to think. I couldn't get the word "no" out. But I couldn't say yes to a lifetime of misery.

"Just give me some time to think, Jen," I told her. "I'll come up with a solution. You know I'll do the best I can for them. It's not that I don't love them. I do. It's just that ... Just let me think, Jen. Let me figure something out."

"Please don't take too long." Her voice was shaking and I could picture her hands trembling as she held the phone to her ear.

I never told Jack about the phone calls. I was afraid he would try to pressure me too. I called Jen a few days later with a plan I had devised. I could try to track down Lily's father's family. Lily's biological father dropped out of sight soon after she turned one. He had come to visit three times, once with a large pink teddy bear, once with a toy phone that had dedicated lines to five Disney Princesses and once with his new puppy, which provided for some great photo opportunities. He was never named on the birth certificate. Jen didn't want to have a permanent tie to him. She wanted autonomy in raising her children the way she thought was best, and child support wasn't worth the risk of having someone meddle in or do some kind of damage to the life she was trying to build. But now that Jen was dying, there had to be a paternal grandmother or aunt or someone who could take Lily. Raising one child, even one with Down Syndrome, would not be as daunting as a sudden house full. I could take Terry and Jimmy and they could have Lily. We could keep the children in touch with frequent visits. This plan would keep everyone out of foster care. Terry and Jimmy would have each other. And Lily would have a much easier time adjusting to the loss of her family members than other children, I reasoned. Her thoughts were simpler, her memory shorter. She would quickly forget the tragedy she just stepped out of and settle fairly quickly into a new life. I thought it was a worthy plan. But Jen protested my trying to contact anyone on the father's side of the family, though she wouldn't tell me why. "It's just not an ideal situation," she said. "Trust me Bev. Leave it alone. Just promise me you'll leave it alone."

Whoever he was, where ever he was and whatever wrong he had done, I wasn't going to find it out from Jen. She remained tenaciously tightlipped.

Meanwhile, she directed my attention to what she viewed as a large body of evidence that caring for Lily is no different from raising any other child.

"I mean, I forget that she has Down Syndrome," Jen said. "Like one time, my friend whose baby is a couple years younger than Lily told me she was worried because her baby bangs his head against the high chair during meals. I told her 'Oh, don't worry. Lily used to do that.' When I hung up the phone, I thought, 'Oh my goodness. How is that comforting to that poor woman?' I had just reassured her that her child is exhibiting the same behaviors as a child with mental retardation."

Jen and I laughed like we hadn't together for a long time.

"Yeah," I said. "I'm sure she slept well that night."

"Yeah," Jen was still chuckling. "But see, to us, Lily is normal. So whatever she does is normal -- at least for Lily."

At the time, I could not figure out what Jen was thinking. Why was she bound and determined to give her kids to someone who didn't want them? Looking back on it, I realize she had more faith in me than I had in myself. But how? How did she know I would rise to the occasion, that I even *could* rise? How did she trust me with her most precious treasure, knowing I didn't value it the way she did? If I would have been her, I would have sooner taken out a classified ad in search of a stranger to take my children than to give them to someone who has made it as clear as I did that I didn't want them. Well, it's not that I didn't want them. It was more that I was scared of them. I was afraid of what they would take away from me. Children don't always bring out the best in you, but there's no way you can get them to adulthood without making at least a few major adjustments in yourself. This I instinctively knew when I said no to those children. I wasn't interested in self improvement.

3

THIEVES OF RAINBOW WHITES

Mom died of breast cancer when Jen and I were in our early 30's. Dad passed away less than two years later of a heart attack. In his time without Mom, Dad was probably the closest to me and Jen that he'd ever been. He was a good man, but he had never been warm by any stretch of the imagination. Jen and I talked about that as she lay in bed, waiting to die. Jack and I had flown out, on a sleety night-flight, to say good-bye to my sister. It was two weeks before Christmas, the children had gone to bed and Jack had gone out to the 24-hour Wal-Mart to buy presents from Jen to the kids. I lay beside Jen with the lights out. We watched the colors dance on the grey ceiling, courtesy of the twinkling lights the neighbors had strung up outside Jen's window, in an effort to provide some small amount of cheer for her last Christmas.

"I went to this parish dance one time when I was in college, and this friend of mine was dancing with her father," Jen said. "I couldn't take my eyes off them. They were so happy and it looked like they must have been chatting about something funny that happened long ago. I remember blinking back tears as I watched them waltz around the floor. Right then, I vowed to marry a man like that some day. A man who'd dance with his daughter."

"Dad wasn't exactly the waltzing type," I agreed.

"No, it's far too sentimental," she said, "and requires, not only touching, but looking into someone's eyes up close for up to three minutes."

"Did you ever resent him?" I asked. "I mean the relationship with him?"

"I used to," Jen said, smoothing the wrinkles out of the sheet on top her flat belly. "Then as I got older, I learned that some other daughter's fathers don't come home at night. And some don't even claim them. And some sneak into their daughters' beds in the middle of the night and put a hand over their mouth and whisper 'shhh' with hot breath in their ears. So I learned to forgive an introverted, hard-shelled, unaffectionate man who never failed to grant any request within his power if it came from one of his children."

"Especially if they professed to believe in Santa Claus," I smiled.

Jen summoned what strength she could for a small laugh. "Yeah. Remember how we used to say we believed in Santa Claus when we were like 12 because Dad said if we stopped believing, he wouldn't come anymore?"

"Yeah, we didn't want that to happen." I said.

"Nope."

The smell of laundry disinfectant wafted into my face as I adjusted the bed covers. It was an odor that couldn't even be overcome by the live pine wreath the hospice nurse brought and hung with red velvet ribbon from the curtain rod of Jen's bedroom window.

"What was your favorite Christmas present?" I asked Jen.

"Oh, that's easy," she said. "Twelve string acoustic. 1982."

"Oh, yeah. You never put that thing down. Much to the dismay of the rest of us who lived with you."

"I wasn't that bad," Jen said, swinging her limp arm at me. Her hand landed on my bicep like a dead fish. "What about you?"

"Hmmm?"

"Your favorite Christmas present," she said.

"Hmmm. I don't know," I said. "There were so many, we-ren't there?"

"Do you think Dad gave us all that stuff to make up for not being able to give us anything emotionally?"

"Why wasn't he able to?" I asked.

"I don't know," Jen said. There was a minute or two of si-lence. "I'm going to see him in a few days. Want me to ask him?"

"A few days?" Where was she getting her information?

"Give or take," she said casually.

I lay there thinking about where the conversation started and remembered that she said she wanted to marry a man who would dance with his daughter.

"Are you sad that you never married, Jen?"

"You know," she adjusted the pillow behind her back with one hand and weakly wriggled her back into it. "I used to pray for a man who would hug me. I just had fantasies of being held. But after the children, I just never needed that anymore. I was holding them and that's really all I needed."

I marveled at her strength.

"Jen, are you scared to die?" I asked.

"Are you?" She turned her head toward my face and searched my eyes for truth.

"I don't know." That wasn't truth.

As a kid, I used to get terribly upset when my parents went away. I would cry like I was grieving -- and I was. I didn't just miss my parents. I was, at a very early age, an accomplished worrier. So if I heard a siren, I automatically assumed it was for them. My parents would always tell me before they left that they wouldn't be gone long because they knew I was heartbroken without them. But they invariably stayed out past the time they said, which made me certain they were in some horrible acci-dent. I don't know to this day why I thought that way -- how I knew to listen for sirens. But it all started after my grandfather died. Our family was staying in our grandfather's house and our parents had to go out to tend to the business of wills and such, leaving us in the care of great-aunt Barbara and other strangers. I remember a wave of panic overtaking me as I wondered if Mom and Dad would ever come back. I found momentary comfort in the realization that my mother had left her purse behind. But then again, my grandfather left everything he owned, and I knew he wasn't coming back for it. At the age of 6, I had touched his stone-cold hand as he lay in his casket and realized death was final. The next day, with distant relatives serving up casseroles and Texas sheet cake at my grandfather's duplex, I cried after my parents for the first time. The tears mixed with the music the neighbor downstairs was playing made me queasy and dizzy. "Don't rock the boat, baby. Don't tip the boat over." To this day, I hate that song. Not that there's much danger of hearing it any-more. I hate foil-wrapped chocolate too because one time before my parents went out to a Christmas party, they gave me a bag of Brach's chocolate bells. My mother explained that they would be back before I knew it. I sat there unwrapping, bell by bell, popping them in my mouth, hoping the sweets would make me feel close to my mother. The more I ate, the farther away my parents felt, until finally, I had binged myself into a nauseated hysteria, listening to the scream of faraway sirens.

Jen's Christmas lights flickered off for several seconds and then resumed their oblivious twinkling. "You're going to die too, you know," Jen said, taking my hand into her soft, cold grasp. "Maybe even before me."

I wrinkled my brow, trying to follow her logic.

"All those high-cholesterol comfort casseroles people keep bringing," she said. "It's hazardous."

"Yeah," I said with a slight smile, which I didn't feel like forming. A long silence followed, with Jen's hand in mine or mine in hers, until I wondered if she had fallen asleep.

"Jen," I whispered.

"Uh-huh?"

"I guess I am scared to die."

"Why?"

"I don't know," I said, squeezing her hand. "I guess I'm afraid of a big black nothingness. Like kids are afraid of the dark."

"But it's not dark," she said. "It's not nothingness."

"What is it?"

"I'm not sure -- exactly." she studied the ceiling and then looked back into my eyes. "Want me to send you a postcard when I get there?"

I let out a small laugh. "So, you're not afraid? At all?"

"I'm afraid of what's going to happen here when I'm gone," Jen said.

****

On Christmas Eve, Jen asked Jack and me to take the children to Mass, which was their family custom. Before we left, Jen took my hand in hers.

"Bev," she said. "Please pray for an answer."

"An answer?"

"About what to do with the kids, Bev." Her eyes were sunken and pleading.

"OK, Jen." I kissed her on the forehead. She closed her eyes and managed a slight smile. Well, I hadn't been much in contact with God, and I didn't exactly know how to start a conversation now. During Mass, I just sat there thinking about how much I was going to miss Jen. She was the only living record of my childhood. After she goes, there will be no one else to say "remember that time we found Mom sitting in the driver's seat of the car in the garage with her suitcase and cosmetic bag, and when we asked her what she was doing she said she was pretending to go on vacation?" Or "remember when Mom got so mad at us for fighting over sugary cereal that she grabbed the Cap'n Crunch and poured it all down the garbage disposal?" Or "remember when we used to wait for Dad to sit down in front of the TV after dinner so we could steal his wintergreen Lifesavers?" I was deep in thought about us rummaging through his brief case and coat pockets looking for those Lifesavers, which, for some strange reason, we called "rainbow whites." A ringing bell, signaling the Consecration, brought me back to my pew and I looked over at the children. Lily had her head lying in Terry's lap and Terry was stroking her hair. On the other side of Lily was Jimmy whose arm was outstretched, resting on her leg, fingers intertwined with hers. It was then I had one of the most lucid moments of my life. And it was nauseating. These three children were about to lose their only parent, and there was no way I was going to let them lose anything else. They had to stay together. Someone was going to have to take all three. Please God, don't let it be me. Was I actually praying?

When we returned from Mass the hospice nurse informed us my baby sister was gone.

I will forever grieve the fact that Jen died with the most important thing in her life unsettled. The last thing I had told her about the future of her children is that I might be able to take Terry and Jimmy. But probably not Lily. I knew we could find a good place for Lily, though, because I had gone on-line and found a website for parents wanting to adopt children with Down Syndrome. I couldn't believe it. Having a disabled child born to you and learning to accept the hand dealt you is one thing. Signing up for trouble is quite another. The fact that there were so many people willing to do this was both comforting and mystifying. But I know it broke Jen's heart to think of her children being split up. I was going to tell her when I returned from Christmas Eve Mass that the thought had broken mine too, but I never got a chance to.

People at the funeral were abundantly kind. As her closest living relative, I was the fortunate receptacle for all the Jen stories people had a need to tell. So many people talked about her generosity. A long line of friends and coworkers streamed by her coffin to say goodbye.

I hate to admit it, but throughout the whole thing, I nursed a secret hope that one of the mourners would introduce himself as Lily's father and beg for custody. Maybe he'd even ask to raise all three children, desiring they be kept together for his daughter's sake. No such man ever surfaced, but the idea of him spans our lives like a phantom burning some kind of indelible mark on our future. Despite the potency of his potential presence, I have grown adept at putting him off. I've done it, in fact, for three decades, half hopeful and half petrified to find him dead by the time I should decide to break my promise and fulfill Lily's request to track him down.

Jen's funeral was probably hardest of all on Lily. I led her by the hand to her mother's side and lifted her up. She looked at her mother and back at me, put her forefinger to her lips and said "shhhhhh." At my prompting, she gently laid a rose on Jen's chest with the other two from Terry and Jimmy. As I started to walk away, Lily stretched out her hands toward her mother and whispered, "Mama." I took her back and she leaned in to give Jen a kiss. Then she put her hand on her mother's shoulder and shook it gently, trying to wake her.

"Let's go, Honey," I said.

"Dow-" she demanded, pointing to the floor.

I put her down and she stood in front of the coffin, looking out at the rest of the room. I told her it was time to go sit down now and give other people a turn to say good-bye to her mother. She said no. I took her by the hand and she slipped her hand back out of mine and planted her bottom on the floor.

"No," she whispered.

Terry noticed what was happening and came to talk her into moving. Lily just shook her head and put her head in her hands. I finally just scooped her up in my arms, and she let out a loud cry, like a baby who is hungry, as I carried her away. Jimmy came rushing over from his seat, where he had been sitting with his elbows propped on his knees and his chin in his hands.

"What's wrong?" he asked.

"She wants to stay with Mama," Terry whispered.

Jimmy put his hand on Lily's back. "It's OK Lily," he told her. "We'll see Mama later."

"Jimmy, Honey, we really should tell Lily the truth about your mother," I whispered. "So she can come to accept it." I had read several books on the topic since I found out Jen was dying.

"I am telling her the truth." Jimmy had eyes the color of the pond adjacent to our backyard where we grew up in Wisconsin. "We'll see her later in Heaven."

Wouldn't it be nice if Jimmy were right, I thought. I missed my sister already, and the thought of never seeing her again was unbearable. What if all my sister's beliefs were not just crutches or superstitions? What if she was experiencing joy beyond measure right this very moment? What if she were kissing the face of God?

I once heard a man, in describing his near-death experience, talk about Heaven as a release from all the emotional and physical pain he didn't even know he had. He said we all go around in this state of suffering, but don't realize it because we have become so accustomed to it -- like people who live for years with backaches. Heaven, he said, relieves all the disregarded pain we unknowingly endure during our imperfect existence on Earth. There were moments in the years to come when I came to realize how this could be so. Before the children came along, if you would have asked me if the glass was half empty or half full, I would have said "Who cares? I'm not thirsty anyway." Today, I will tell you the glass is filled to the brim and I would give anything for a sip.

4

UNTIL LILY

It was a good six months before Lily stopped asking where Jen was. She used a series of made-up signs and the word Mama to find out if her mother was still sleeping and if so, where? And -- if I can be so presumptuous as to claim to read her mind -- "Why doesn't someone go wake Mama up so things can get back to normal around here?"

The day we went to court and I heard the judge pronounce us a family, a wave of queasy dread rushed over me. I felt like a fire jumper, those crazy guys who parachute from an airplane into a forest to fight a raging blaze. If the wind shifts and the fire starts coming at them, there's no way out. That's what it felt like taking on these three children. The wildfire was coming at me.

And yet, even for all my pessimism, I had underestimated the difficulty of what lay ahead. I never could have imagined how hard it would be. I have to be honest and say, if I had, I would have run. Very fast. And very far. I wasn't the type who could have weathered such hardships. I wasn't. But somehow I came to be.

There were days when the exasperation would build up so much pressure in my throat that I was afraid it would blow my head clean off my shoulders. One of those times was the day I had somehow managed to get all the laundry clean -- even all the renegade socks that had escaped under the beds and the underwear that had been shoved behind dressers by their owners who thought it more efficient to hide them than to make eleven extra steps to the bathroom laundry bin. So there it was, on the large leather couch, focal point of the family room -- a beautiful monument to domestic skill: Clean clothes, folded and stacked into towering piles, sorted by drawer of destination. It had been a two-day undertaking to get to this point, one day for collecting and washing, the next for ironing and folding. I had been able to reunite socks that hadn't had mates in maybe three years. It was pretty pathetic how much joy it brought me to see them bundled and piled like firewood before the first snow. I had a nagging feeling when I left the room, something was going to happen to my masterpiece. What I couldn't have predicted was how dreadful that something would be. Apparently Lily, upon seeing the clean underwear, suddenly realized that hers were not and decided to make a trade. One pair of underwear full of poop in exchange for a freshly laundered pair. In the process, unbeknownst to her I assume, she had parked her bare soiled bottom on top of the other clean piles of clothes, presumably trying to find a comfortable spot to make the swap. I'm just glad the plumber was there that day. If I had been alone in the house with that child, I might have killed her.

Jen had Lily almost potty trained before she died. But you still had to "remind" her to go. By remind, I mean, you had to drag her into the bathroom and wrestle her onto the toilet and listen to her scream at you until she went. Sometimes, when I just wasn't up for the fight, I would decide to wait until she was willing to go. This never happened and invariably that tactic resulted in a big mess to clean up. This is when I would lose my patience with her because I knew she was just being stubborn. Then, she hated being cleaned up and would cry about it the whole time. "It's no fun for me either," I would tell her. "Can't you feel the poop coming out? Can't you stop yourself and run to the potty?" We got through that stage and then she'd only occasionally have a week here and there of relapse. Usually it was because she was sick -- like with a cold or something. Now that I struggle with the same malady, I feel terrible for having scolded her. I'm sure if she could have controlled it, she would have, it feels so awful. Sometimes I catch a look on a nurse's face and I know what she is thinking because I had the same thoughts. "This butt is too big for wiping." There's a reason they show behinds on Huggies commercials but not on Depends ads.

Last night, I had horrible intestinal cramps and rang for someone to help me to the bathroom. I must have rung for the nurse five or six times, at least. The cramps were getting progressively worse until I couldn't stand it anymore, so I decided to get myself to the bathroom as quickly as I could. I didn't want anyone else to have to clean up the mess that might ensue if I waited one more minute. I wheeled myself to the bathroom door jam and pushed myself up on the arms of the chair. As I did, another wave of cramps hit me and the whole weight of my body rushed to my shoulders, pushing me forward, face first, onto the cold tiles. I screamed out and lay there hoping it was one of the nice nurses who found me, although at this point, I would have settled for Benito Mussolini or even Nurse Gilda. I heard footsteps, and a pair of white shoes appeared below my eyes. There was a heavy sigh, and a couple of large hands grabbed me under my armpits, hoisted me up and plunked me into my wheelchair with all the care you would take with a bag of cement. It was Nurse Gilda.

"Mrs. Greeley, you've been told not to get out of your chair without help," she said grunting through the weight she had to lift.

"I rang for help," I said. "No one came."

"You need to be patient and give us a minute to get here." Her voice was coarse. This is not the way she would be talking if a supervisor was within earshot.

"A minute?" I said. "It was fifteen. I couldn't wait any longer. I had to go."

"Mrs. Greeley, you are wearing a diaper." She said it like an accusation.

"Nurse Lowe, I prefer not to use it," I snapped. "I prefer to use the toilet, just like all other humans who have passed the age of three."

"Well, you didn't make it anyway, did you?" She had the tone of spoiled adolescence, a bleached-blonde, sports-car-driving teenager rubbing it in for having beaten someone out of the lead part in a school play.

"I'd like to know, Nurse, do you enjoy being ugly to people or can you just not help yourself?"

I couldn't believe that came out of my mouth. Normally I avoid bridge burning at this stage in my life. Everyone else, after all, holds the key to my sanity, and that sanity depends on the most inane things -- like getting to the toilet in time. I am at the mercy of all. And mercy, I'm learning, if it comes at all, comes in limited quantities around here.

The nurse said nothing as she went about cleaning me up. Her motions were crisp and curt, in her effort to give expression to her forbidden enmity. The shower would have felt good, but I couldn't enjoy it, knowing there was someone fuming on the other side of the curtain. Even if I hardly knew her or cared about what she thought, it still gave me the creeps to think she and I were stuck with each other. Neither one of us could go storming from the room in a silent, sour vow never to speak to each other again. Her shift was twelve hours long and then there would someday be another one.

But nonverbal hostility was nothing new to me. About six months after Jen died, Lily began to develop quite a temper. Most of her protests came in the form of very unpleasant noises. To show her dislike at the smallest offense, she would walk up to the laundry room door, which was always closed, open it, slam it back again and stomp off. Without words to tell me where to go, slamming and screaming became her primary means of communication. I know it must have been frustrating to have desires that no one would ever meet. Lily probably thought we were all callous, insensitive ogres -- or idiots -- be-cause most of the time she probably wasn't asking for anything unreasonable. Her wants were always pretty simple. The pink cup. Watch the show again. Find the *Barbie and the Twelve Dancing Princesses* book that we read the night before.

Sometimes Terry and Jimmy could figure it out and avert a nasty incident. They had a historical perspective on Lily that I lacked. Plus, they understood her primitive sign language, which she herself had made up. But trying to guess what this nonverbal child wanted wasn't the most difficult part of taking care of her. It was being screamed or spit at when I guessed wrong. So half the time, I didn't even try.

I used to read all of Jen's bylines online. It had become such a habit that, after she died, I logged on to read her replacement's columns. I e-mailed her often and she was always happy to talk to me because she had been close to Jen. One day, Calli Flannery wrote a column about a day she spent in a mental institution. When she got there, they issued her headphones that would feed a continuous thread of chatter into her ear. The unnerving device was meant to replicate what it is like for a schizophrenic who hears voices inside her head. I e-mailed her and told her that if she wanted to see real insanity, she should come spend a day at our house. "By the way," I wrote, "where can I get a pair of those headphones? It might be a nice change from the kids yelling at me."

In addition to being miserable at home, Lily was miserable at her new school too. I would get reports from the teacher that she had thrown something across the room or scratched or bit another student. Jen had told me Lily was stubborn and had a bit of a temper, but she never mentioned anything like this. One day, I realized that the anger started right around the time she stopped asking about Jen. I think she finally accepted the fact that her mother wasn't coming back. That's when the fury set in. I wasn't sure what to do. It's very difficult to explain things to someone who has questions but can't ask them. Was she wondering why her mother went away? Was she wondering why people die? Was she wondering if other people would start dying too? I decided I would have to address all the questions she may have just in case I hit on one of them. One Saturday afternoon, I took her out for ice cream. I waited until she was done with her cone and then I said, "Lily, you know that your Mama died." She nodded.

"And you know she's not coming back?"

She just looked at me, sort of puzzled.

"When someone dies, Lily, you can't see them again. They don't come back."

"No." she said. Sort of a question.

"But I'm going to take care of you now."

She nodded.

"You and Terry and Jimmy live with me now and I'll take care of you."

She nodded and smiled slightly.

"I will be like your Mama."

"Mama," she said, smiling wide now.

From that day forward, she called me Mama and eventually Mommy. She couldn't say Auntie Bev anyway, which is what Terry and Jimmy continue to call me to this day.

After the ice cream talk, the incident reports from school gradually decreased and she became a student with model behavior. She even got student of the week in her school, where she spent the majority of her day in classes with typical students. I had to put up a bit of a fight to get the school to agree to put her in regular classes because it's more work for them. They had to assign her an aid to help her through many of the subjects. It's much easier and cheaper to have all special needs student in one room with a small team of teachers and aides to educate them. But we tried Lily in one of those resource classrooms and she was miserable. I never found out why, but I knew she couldn't stay there.

****

About a year after the kids moved in with us, they began lobbying for a dog. It started as Terry's dream, but soon she had enlisted Jimmy and even Jack to pester me as well. And every time someone would talk about getting a dog, which was at least two dozen times a day, Lily would look at me with raised eyebrows and slap her leg, which is a sign she had learned for "dog." It seemed overwhelming to me to take on one more thing that needed my attention. But I promised the children if they got good grades, we would get a cat. Their studies had understandably suffered a bit since Jen passed away and I thought they could use a little incentive. I also was hedging my bets that they couldn't pull their grades up all that quickly. Well, they must have really wanted an animal because the next grading period, they got all A's and B's, with the exception of Jimmy's C in math. So off we went to the pound. There weren't a lot of declawed cats to choose from. I really didn't like cats all that much. I had no good memories of them from childhood and two particularly bad ones. One is a vague recollection of my aunt's cat Buster who scratched me once on the back of the hand when I tried to pet him. The other is a vivid memory of a skinny white cat with icy blue eyes who was the family pet of the boy I baby sat. Any time I glanced at that venomous animal, she would hiss and snaaah at me. She gave me the creeps, and I had what I thought were irrational fears of her pouncing on my neck and biting out my adam's apple if I ever were to happen to fall asleep there. One evening after the boy had gone to bed, I was sitting in the reclining chair watching TV. I reached down to scratch my ankle or something and suddenly, I felt something sharp slice my skin. The cat, who was apparently hiding inside the chair waiting for her opportunity, reached up through the gap in the upholstery and scratched my arm. I was so shocked, I quickly closed the chair. After washing up the scratch, I considered letting the cat out, but I feared she would come at me with a vengeance. She was making no protests, so I hadn't felt any urgency, but it was nearing time for the boy's parents to come home, and it had been close to two hours since the chair incident. I started to wonder what kind of hardware was inside a reclining chair. Could the cat have been killed instantly when the chair closed? How would I explain that to Ice Queen's owners? I finally got the courage to pull the lever on the footrest, and the cat bolted straight out of the room. She never looked back, and I never agreed to babysit at that house again.

The lady at the pound said it was best to get a cat that still had its claws. She said de-clawed cats are insecure with their environment because they have no way of defending themselves. I guess that made sense, but I still wanted a cat that wouldn't slice open a baby sitter's forearm. I also worried about Lily. I wasn't quite sure how she would treat an animal. Would she try to pick it up by its head, put pantyhose on it, hold it down and spoon feed it spinach? In my mind, the more defenseless the animal, the safer Lily was going to be. And the safer the cat would ultimately be because it was going to end up right back here on kitty death row if it so much as looked at us funny. Of course, none of the cats were there because they had scratched anyone or ripped apart the sofa upholstery or climbed the curtains. No, these were all perfect felines, whose heartbroken owners had to say goodbye for the sake of their asthmatic children. I had no idea before visiting the pound what an epidemic asthma had become. Of course, all the dogs where there because their owners were moving to an apartment that doesn't allow pets.

We ended up bringing home a cat whose claws were intact because that's the one the children fell in love with. It was a beautiful cat named Sunset. Orange and fat with green eyes. But I can't say having claws made him any more secure. For the first two weeks we never saw him. He staked out a hiding place under my bed. The children tried to bait him out with tuna fish and feathers taped to drinking straws. I wouldn't let them stick their hands under the bed and I wasn't about to try to pull him out, so there he stayed. Until one morning, I came into the kitchen and found Sunset and Lily under the table. That cat was actually letting her pet him. After that, he warmed up a little to the rest of the family. But Lily's were the only hands he ever permitted on him for more than 30 seconds at a time. Maybe because she moved slowly and she was predictable, unlike the other two children.

As disenchanted as I am by cats, I am indebted to that one. Lily had never been able to make a "K" sound before Sunset. "Kitty" had become her new favorite word. That's what she called him most of the time, except during bedtime prayers. She would make the sign of the cross and say "Mama, Sun-sun, Terry, Sun-sun, Jim, Sun-sun, Lily, Sun-sun." Then she'd make the sign of the cross again and say "Amen." There must have been something to all that praying because that cat lived well into Lily's 20's. Lily stayed in her room for a week and cried when Sunset died. On the eighth day, I went and got her a black kitten, which won her over the minute she held it to her face and it gnawed on her earlobe. She was able to take Midnight with her when she moved into the group home. The cat became instant friends with the old black dog without eyes that already lived there. The previous owner set the dog on fire and he lost his eyes to an infection that set in due to the burns. He does just fine without his vision as long as he stays around the house, I guess because of a dog's amazing senses of smell and hearing. His name is Jasper and Lily talks about him all the time. Probably as much as she talks about the people, most of whom are young with mild to moderate mental disabilities. The couple who runs the group home is good folk, in their late 50's probably. They seemed so happy to get Lily. They took her to the store with them and let her pick out the wallpaper for her room before she moved in. They had to do quite a bit of work on it after the last resident took a key and carved the upper-case alphabet, his version of a United States map and the American flag into the drywall. When I asked them how he had done such extensive damage without their noticing it, they said they knew he was working on it and just let him continue his month's-long project because it was a creative endeavor, and it gave him something to do. Walls are easy to fix, they said. I figure any couple with that kind of outlook would have more than enough patience for Lily.

I know they say once a parent, always a parent, and that even when your children are grown, you are still responsible for them, you still worry about them and there's a good chance that you'll be coming to their assistance more than once past their 18th birthday. But no one really knows what it's like to be a perpetual parent unless they have raised a child with mental retardation. The condition stretches the entire process out and there one day comes a realization that all the struggles are not going to end any time soon -- if ever. For me, that realization came at Barnes & Noble. Right before leaving for the book store, I had told one of my friends on the phone that I could handle everything but the screaming. Since Lily couldn't talk, the only way she had of communicating her displeasure was to scream at the top of her lungs and hope that someone would be adequately annoyed and give her what she wanted. Any forward-thinking parent knows not to give into that, just as you don't give into the 2-year-old who uses that same tactic. But remember a typical 2-year-old is progressing at a speedy rate and will move onto new tactics once he realizes that particular strategy doesn't work. Children with Down Syndrome are going to linger there for a while. All of this I intuitively knew, so I didn't expect the problem to go away overnight. I was, however, shocked by this spectacle in the bookstore. A woman in her mid-50's was walking ten paces ahead of a young woman with Down Syndrome, whom I thought was about 20, screaming at her mother "Mama, Mama, Mama." Everyone in the store, I'm sure, thought that the daughter was yelling because she wanted her mother to slow down and that her mother was so insensitive, she refused to walk at her disabled daughter's pace. Me, I knew, what was going on. That mother was trying to get away from the screaming she had put up with for two decades. And right there I saw a flash-forward of me and Lily. I was going to share a fate with this other poor mother. Our children were going to scream at us until the end of eternity and there was nothing we could do about it. There is only so fast you can walk to get away from your child.

Then at some point, when the distance gets too great, you have to turn around and go back again, whether you want to or not.

My prediction was, happily, inaccurate and Lily did not spend the rest of her life screaming at me.

There were so many habits I thought she would never outgrow. Some I just gave up on. Like the shoving of enormous amounts of food in her mouth, presumably because the weak muscle tone made the food undetectable to the muscles inside her mouth. Then there was the very consistent practice of putting her shoes on the wrong feet.

"Wrong foot," I'd say. Then she'd take them off, swap them and look up at me with question marks in her eyes. As if there was a third choice of how to put your shoes on. And then there were days when I was just too tired, or too frustrated or too late to tell her that her shoes were on the wrong feet. I thought for sure she'd notice something didn't feel quite right after an hour or two, but she never did.

Having no training at all in how to raise children, much less special needs children, I probably expected too much. There are moments in the life of every parent, I'm sure, when you are absolutely certain that the behavior you are witnessing is the precursor to a life of deranged crime. If you could just know that these phases will pass, the pharmaceutical companies who produce medications treating anxiety, high blood pressure, ulcers, headaches, heart attacks and insanity could close up shop. But parents don't know from moment to moment if they are dealing with something typical and benign or whether Ted Bundy's mother would share similar stories of her boy growing up. Thinking things are going to get easier with some on-the-job training is simply naive because each child is a wholly different creation and each minute ushers in a new and different crisis.

And some of the same old ones as well. I know this seems like a trivial thing, but it was really quite a problem that Lily had this way of making her armpits disappear when she didn't want to be picked up. People with Down Syndrome have super flexible joints. I have baby pictures of Lily sleeping with her feet up by her ears, her legs perfectly straight. It's what makes it harder for them to learn to walk and it's why they move through the world slower than everyone else. Well, not everyone. There are always us old folks with Parkinson's. At least my mind hasn't slowed down yet, which is good enough for 78 years old. I've always been one of those "things could be worse" kind of people. I don't know why that mantra never saw me through when it came to Lily. I allowed myself to be tormented by the things she couldn't do or did slower or didn't do as well. I spent my life watching her and wondering what could be the reason for all this? Was all this really necessary? I suppose if I were the metaphysical type I would have come up with some theory -- like there's a unique role, a certain need in the universe for a Lily-ness that only Lily can fill. This wondering and always being perplexed and vexed was something new for me since Lily. I had been neither a seeker of truth nor a pilgrim on a journey. Just a used book dealer, who came home every evening to her three-bedroom home, poured a cup of Seattle's Best, popped the foot rest and read the latest best-selling memoir. A philosopher I was not. Not until Lily.

So Jack and I muddled through, each in our own way, each in a way that made the other crazy. He used to say I liked to borrow trouble. He thought I was always looking for something to get all over the kids about. Jack had this placid, detached technique that the kids loved. When I had to go out, I always wondered if the house would still be standing when I got home. The difference between Jack and me was this: If I'm in charge and a kid picks up a match, I immediately take the match away, sit the kid down and give him a 15-minute lecture on the dangers of matches, drag him to the internet to look up fire safety, garner six weeks of his allowance to pay for medical bills of burn victims and make him write "I will never play with matches" 50 times in his neatest hand writing. If Jack is in charge, on the other hand, we will all end up standing in a smoking pile of charred rubble with the so-called head of the household asking "OK, now, what have we learned from this?" I suppose we could have made a good team if we would have seen and understood that we balanced each other out. But children are a very difficult thing to compromise on. You simply can't let the other person have his or her way if you think your child will become an arsonist because of it. So arguments ensue. Many of ours ensued in front of the children, which I regret. Jimmy used to try to ease the tension at such times by doing thoughtful little things, like bringing us cool drinks or tidying the pillows on the couch. Terry would slip off into a book or silently escape into a miniature world of plastic animals. She either pretended not to notice or she was oblivious to the fighting. I always assumed it was the former, because she was never oblivious to anything else. Lily would walk up to one of us, try to get eye contact and say "Hi." She would do this 10 or 15 times throughout the tiff, seemingly testing to make sure she hadn't become the object of our outrage. All three children would be on their best behavior through the entire quarrel and often up to a half hour after. I'm assuming they either felt responsible for causing a rift between us or they thought one of our heads would explode if they added any more aggravation to our angst. I feel sorry that we made them feel they had it within their power to send us over the edge, but I have to hand it to them for having the decency not to.

The differences between mine and Jack's parenting styles were particularly apparent in public places. At some point during an outing, Lily would show her displeasure with us by plopping herself down in the middle of the floor, taking off her shoes and refusing to respond to any of our requests. So as to avoid a scene, Jack would enter into negotiations and promise her all things short of a Falabella pony if she came into quiet compliance. Now, I heard somewhere you should never negotiate with terrorists, so I would have preferred that he pick her up in a fireman hold and whisk her to the car. If she screamed all the way there, so be it. Eventually, she would learn her technique wasn't going to work.

Eventually, of course, never comes soon enough. No one quite gets it in the beginning. When children with Down Syndrome are small, you can't possibly know the amount of work involved in the next 20 years. You're in for the same ludicrous behavior we've all come to expect from little kids, but it comes at you encased in increasingly bigger bodies. After they reach a certain body mass, brute force is no longer an option. You must learn to outsmart your opponent. You can't, for instance, pick up an 80-pound kid throwing a tantrum in the middle of the cereal aisle, hike her over your shoulder and head for the door. But you can break out into the chorus of her favorite Cocoa Crunchies commercial in hopes of confusing her long enough with your willingness to make a fool of yourself that she forgets what she was throwing a fit about.

I had a few good years with the older two until the teen years hit and things got kind of rocky. I recognized that as a normal part of life, since I myself did that to my parents. I guess I made some mistakes in how I handled things with Terry and Jimmy, and we never really recovered the ground we had lost. As young adults they remained distant, I assumed almost resentful, though they never really said as much. I don't know why they would be. I think things got better between us after they had their own children and realize how many mistakes parents make in a given day. Or hour. Lily never went through the typical teen rebellion. She continued to grow more attached to me. More loving and, I guess I would say, humble. She never wanted to leave my side. I know part of that was because the world is so uncertain for people like her. It's not that most people are intentionally cruel. It's just the logistics of dealing with her disabilities. Like who is going to be able to decipher what she is saying, other than her family and those skilled at understanding someone talking to them from inside a deep well with marshmallows stuffed in her mouth. Not that we got through Lily's teen years without incident. She showed her independence by insisting on doing the thing she'd been told not to -- over and over and over again. Like calling 911 when there was clearly no emergency. Then again, maybe she just enjoyed the lights and sirens too much to control herself. Or the police officers. So this continued -- once a month or so for nearly a year, until I asked a policeman to respond to the 911 call by putting handcuffs on Lily and placing her in his squad car. If she hadn't been so repentant -- sobbing like a baby -- he might have had to drive her to the station to make his point, but she was already scared enough. It was probably the most brilliant consequence I ever came up with. Lily didn't dial 911 again until 18 years later, when she found me face down on the kitchen floor. But only after she threw herself on top of me and commanded me to make a full and immediate recovery.

"Mommy, Mommy, you have to get up," she sobbed into my back. "You can- jus- lay there. Who be my frien-?"

I think that must have been the first moment Lily understood that I am not immortal. She had endured losses before, but they had not presented themselves in her child-like sanguine psyche as any sort of a trend.

She wasn't the only one coming to a grim realization. I had always known Lily would be orphaned again someday, but I had not expected it to happen so soon. I had planned to live into my 80s. I lay there wishing I was younger, wishing our family was larger, wishing I knew someone whose life was set up to wrap its arms around Lily's, embracing all the peril and delight therein. The lives of Lily's siblings do not meet that criterion.

I lay there in that moment, paralyzed in body, flailing in mind. Why did Jen have to make this so difficult? I uttered a silent plea. "Please, Jen, if I live to see another day, give me permission to break my promise. Surely, by now, you must realize I made a promise that should not be kept. What could be so dreadful about the man you had once chosen to love? If truly there is but a thin veil between Heaven and Earth, let me hear your answer."

I heard nothing but the lamentations of approaching sirens.

5

MATCHES AND STEAK KNIVES

When I was first diagnosed with Parkinson's Disease, I read an article about care-giver burnout. It talked about how people who take care of Parkinson's patients can say things they later regret. I gave each of the children a copy of the article and I told them that whatever they might say to me when I'm at my most burdensome is completely forgiven. I read the article to Lily. She said, "I never never be mad at you, Mommy. It not your fault your sick." I smiled and thought that someday, she would understand. To this day, I don't think she does. I really don't think she ever will. Lily actually enjoys taking care of me, which is why I don't feel bad about asking her for help. I try to feed myself breakfast and lunch, but I often don't get much down and I lose what little appetite I started with before I'm through. I'm so worn out by the end of the day, I can't get the fork from the plate to my mouth. I'm always happy to let Lily feed me dinner. On meat loaf nights, I don't give her much trouble. But tonight is roast beef and the texture makes me think of cows, which is not necessarily what you want to think of when you eat beef.

"Do you wanna bite uh peas?" she asks, holding the fork, with two peas on it to my mouth.

"Yes, please, Darling."

"Now, do you wanna bite uh rice?"

"Yes, please."

"Now, do you wanna bite uh meat?"

"No thank you."

"Rice?"

"Yes, please."

"Then eat a bite uh meat." She sticks the fork into the shreds of flesh and holds it to my mouth.

"No, thank you."

"C'mon," she says, cheerfully, refusing to budge the fork. "Bite uh meat."

"No, thank you."

"I cut it smaller."

"Smaller? It's practically puree."

Her fingers are chubby like sausages wrapped around the knife. She rests her tongue between her lips as she saws at the meat. The fork, now in her left hand, makes a wide arc before it reaches my lips. My pity for Lily's lack of coordination moves me, and I decide if she put that much effort into getting it to my mouth, the least I can do is eat it.

"How's that?" she asks, dabbing my mouth with a napkin.

"Fine, Honey."

"Do you want your pudding?"

"OK. Sure."

"Have two more bites of meat." That was an old trick that always worked with Lily when she was little and counted carbo-hydrates most prized among all pleasures. It was amazing the healthy things she would agree to eat in order to get a slice of buttered bread. I usually had to stick the vegetables in her mouth myself to get her to eat them because her hands refused to be coerced by my nutritional blackmail. But her mouth was willing.

For a short time, there was one exception to the rule of carbs, when I didn't have to trick her mouth into opening. Lily would eat any free sample at Costco, even if it was protein. Probably even if it was protein in the form of a grub worm, though I never did test that theory. She would go nuts at the sight of a toaster oven and a tray of toothpicks and gobble up any ethnicity or consistency of food served by a senior citizen wearing plastic gloves and a hair net. Then she would beg for more, which of course, is out of the question, unless you're willing to dip into your 401K to finance the purchase. If your child should happen to ask for seconds, you will quickly learn that every free sample distributor has apparently received special training in eliminating freeloading through nonverbal cynicism, specifically a scowl, followed by a sideways glance that, if it could talk, would say, "Oh, you've trained your child to whine for more, have you? Well, I didn't fall off the turnip truck yesterday, Dearie. You've come here to make a meal off these morsels, just admit it." So to prove those accusations wrong and expand Lily's repertoire of food she would not scream at me for serving, I would have to make the investment in the 10-pound bag of boneless chicken wings, the 320-count box of taquitos or the drum of hummus. I'd get it home and, of course, Lily would refuse to touch it ever again. So one day, when she begged me to buy the teriyaki chicken bowls after sampling a tablespoon of it, I felt like I had to justify my cruel decision to ignore my poor little child's request for nourishment. "She'll eat anything in sample size," I told the free sample lady. "But she won't eat it at home."

"I can give you some of these little cups to serve it in," she offered.

I walked away chuckling, but when I got home, I cut Lily's hamburger into tiny pieces and stuck a toothpick in each bite. She gobbled them up. From then on I served virtually everything with any kind of nutritional value on a stick or in a dixie cup, and smiled to myself when she asked for refills of such undesirable dishes as glazed carrots or baked chicken. That phase lasted about six months and then even a toothpick did not provide enough incentive and we had to move on to other gimmicks.

"Wanna play cards?" Lily asks, spooning a bite of tapioca pudding into my mouth.

"OK."

"Uno?"

"Yeah, sure," I say. "I think I'm done eating, Lily, and I need to use the little girls' room." My intestines were starting to cramp and I suddenly had that woozy feeling.

The next thing I remember, I was waking from a dream about Mary, the mother of Jesus. She was sweeping a dirt floor, and she was pregnant. As she worked, she hummed in rhythm with the brush strokes of the broom. As I regained full consciousness, I realized Mary's humming was actually Lily's words, muffled by the sheets on top my belly, where she had laid her head. "Hail Mary, hail Mary, hail Mary, hail Mary, hail Mary, hail Mary, hail Mary, hail Mary, hail Mary, hail Mary, Glory Be. Our Father. Hail Mary, hail Mary, hail Mary..." She was moving her fingers along the beads of a Rosary. This is the way Terry had taught Lily to say the Rosary when she was small. Lily was swinging her foot back and forth, scuffing the floor with the sole of her shoe. That is what, in my dream, my brain had turned into the sound of Mary's sweeping.

One of the nurses explained to me that my blood pressure had dropped and I had passed out. I had dealt with low blood pressure all my life. In my younger years, I could never stand up too quickly unless my ears would ring and a multi-colored snow would fall over my eyes. It had never been a big problem, but it is ultimately what landed me in this place. It only took my passing out once while the stove was on to send Terry on a frenetic search for a nursing home and an attorney to help sign my life over to strangers.

Poor Jim and Terry. It's hard enough telling an old lady she isn't fit enough to live in her house anymore. It's another telling a young woman with Down Syndrome that she will have to move out of the family home and start a new life without her mother. Terry had done the research to find a place for me and Jim found a group home for Lily. Everyone cried that day, except for me, because I don't cry. But if I did, tears would certainly have come. This was the last time I would ever see my home. People who go into nursing homes don't come out. This, to me, was the end of my life. I had visited enough friends in

nursing homes over the years to know that your whole life is reduced to a space the size of yourself when you're holding your
breath. I took nothing with me that couldn't fit in half of a closet.
I took nothing with me of value, not even if it were small enough
to fit in half a closet, because it would probably be stolen. All
the stuff you've accumulated, you watch it all go into the dump-
ster or into the hands of strangers at a garage sale. Lily wanted to
keep everything. Anytime we put something in a box, we'd
catch her swiping it back out when no one was watching. She'd
say it was the "one thing" she always really loved and she
wanted it as a keepsake. We told her she can't keep everything --
only as much as will fit in her five crates. So she'd go rummaging through to take something out so she could fit the new thing
she'd fallen in love with all over again after two decades of never noticing it. Fortunately, Terry and Jimmy have a tremendous
amount of patience with her. They had taken a week off of work
to get us packed and moved. Halfway through the process it was
looking like they needed more like a month. How do you disas-
semble 76 years of life in seven days? By the end, we were just
looking for excuses to trash things. "Look, that Renoir has a
crack in the corner of the frame. That's no good. Get rid of it.
And look this old Stradivarius has a missing string. Throw it
away." The toughest things were those you couldn't sell or even
give away and you hated to throw away because they had attached themselves to a memory. Like the old Chianti bottles
turned candle holders. Each of the children had made one by letting various colors of candles drip down over the bottle. They
weren't works of art, but they represented a rite of passage, because if you were allowed to make one it meant you were trusted
to light a match.

Matches and steak knives were big deals in our house. At
every birthday we celebrated, Terry would beg me to let her
light the candles on the cake. Finally when she was 10, I let her
light her own. It was that same year I let her cut a tomato with a
steak knife and I taught her to turn on the gas stove. So I asked

her one night, "You're 10 now. Do you think you could live alone if you had to?"

"Sure, I'm independent."

"Well, you can't drive. How would you get groceries?"

"Safeway.com?"

"Would you be able to take a city bus somewhere?"

"I don't know. Why are you asking all these questions?"

"Well, I read somewhere that the average person with Down Syndrome is about as smart as a 10-year-old, so I was just wondering how independent Lily is going to be when she's grown up?"

"Well, I'm pretty smart," Terry said.

She really was.

"Could you take a city bus to the mall?" I asked.

"Uh, probably not." She raised an eyebrow. "But it would be fun to try."

"Don't get any ideas," I said, mussing her hair.

****

The day the children moved me in here, I had a horrible headache. The place reeked of urine and Pine-Sol. The imagination inside my nostrils told me this, even though I had long ago lost my sense of smell. As Lily led my shuffling feet across the grey linoleum, I remember thinking, this is the only floor I will ever see again. Looking back now, I realize Lily's hand in mine that day was meant to send a clear message. Terry walked ahead of us and Jimmy behind. Terry was now the leader of the family, Jimmy was backing her up, supporting her decisions from a distance. Lily was right beside me and she would never leave -- not of her own will anyway.

I felt like a small child that day. It was on that day, with Lily's hand in mine, that all the memories of her first day of kindergarten came flooding through. We hadn't been together for very long, but it was long enough for her not to want to be away from me and placed in the hands of strangers. She covered one

56

eye with each of her two thumbs and buried her face in my spandex stretch slacks when the teacher tried to befriend her. "That's a beautiful dress, Lily." Mrs. Ethelbaum stooped to tell her. "Is pink your favorite color?"

I wondered what Lily was afraid of. She looked like a nice enough woman to me. The classroom was bursting with primary colors and pictures of animals drawn in a close-to-cartoon style. The floor-to-ceiling giraffe wore a big letter G around his neck. All the other animals were pretty much to scale, except the ant crawling through the hole in the letter A. He would have been about the size of a gerbil. I pointed the horse out to Lily, remembering that Jen had told me Lily had been on a horse many times. She had taken hippo therapy for a while to improve her balance and coordination. But the drawing of the horse in Mrs. Ethelbaum's classroom offered nothing to impress Lily and she shook her head and returned her face to my thigh.

I stooped to talk to her, but she closed her eyes. "I'm going to go now for a little while, and you're going to stay here and have fun with Mrs. Ethelbaum and some new friends, and I'll be back very soon to get you, OK?"

"No." She shook her head.

"Mrs. Greeley, nice to meet you." The woman in a navy blue blazer, pencil skirt and red patent-leather pumps bent slightly at the hip and stretched out her hand. Her voice brought me back to the present -- from the aroma of crayons to the imaginary stench of ammonia. She was tall and thin, with dark hair pulled back so tight, it looked as though her smile was permanently stretched onto her face. I reached out my hand and placed it in hers. "I'm Claudia Vasquez." she said. "I'm the social worker here. You let me know if there is anything you need. I'm here to make sure everything is going smoothly for you."

"Thank you." I nodded slightly.

"She nice," Lily said as Ms. Vasquez made her way down the hall into the administrative office.

A tall and thin young man in a crisp white uniform smiled at us as he pushed an elderly man in a wheelchair past.

"He nice too," Lily said.

"Yeah, the staff here seems great," said Terry.

"I love doctors," Lily said. "I think Daddy is a doctor."

"Really?" I said. "Did your Mama tell you that?"

"No."

"Did your Mama tell you anything about your Daddy?"

"No. But I know everything. He love me from his heart."

Jimmy sat surveying the ceiling, checking out lighting or the fire sprinklers or the smoke detectors or maybe just checking out. He has done that ever since he was small. Jack and I used to have to talk a combination of Pig Latin and sign language if we wanted to hold a conversation over Terry's head and she would still figure it out. Jimmy could be in the same room, doing nothing but watching dust dance in a stream of sunlight, and he wouldn't hear a word. One time Terry came into the room after watching Les Miserable and wanted to know why the inn keeper's wife had called him an "S-H-I-T," which, seeing Jimmy in the room, she spelled so he wouldn't hear the forbidden word. I was livid.

"Terry," I said. "What grade is Jimmy in?"

"Third."

"Right. And third graders can spell."

"I'm sorry, Auntie," she said. "I wasn't thinking."

"And what do third grade boys like to do if they hear a word they're not supposed to say?"

"I don't know." Terry shrugged.

"They like to run around the world for the next six months saying it over and over and over again," I informed her.

"I'm sorry, Auntie."

Fortunately, this entire conversation transpired unnoticed by Jimmy, including my reaming Terry out through clenched teeth. So we didn't have to worry about that word making it into his vocabulary and onto a pink slip for another three years.

6

THE SHADOWS OF WINDMILLS

I tried to raise the children the way Jen would have liked. There were things I would have eased up on if they were my children from the start. But if I thought it was something she would say no to, I usually said no. And I felt it a duty to take them to church occasionally. Terry would beg to go to Mass and I would break down every six or eight weeks and take them. Even though I had long ago lost my faith I didn't see any reason why they should. But the biggest thing is I know Jen would have wanted them to go to church. I would always sit in the pew and feel guilty. "If you really exist, God, you made a big mistake. Jen should have been here with her children. I could have died relatively unnoticed. Jack would have grieved for a while, but he would have moved on and remarried. The store would have been sold to someone else who would have run it pretty much the way I did, minus a few too many clearance sales owing to my disdain for clutter. So what was the deal with her dying of cancer instead of me? And why am I sitting here in church, talking to a God I don't believe in?" Well, what else should I be doing? I am at church, after all.

I know, when it came to religion, I was always somewhat of a puzzle to the children. Terry would ask me why I didn't say the prayers at church. I told her I'd forgotten them. Twelve years later, Lily asked me the same thing. I told her the same thing.

59

She saved up her money for six months and bought me a book of Christian Prayers for my birthday.

After a while, Terry stopped asking to go to Mass, but Lily never did. In addition to trying to do what would make my sister happy, I guess I was making somewhat of a Pascal's Wager. If by chance the stories about Jesus are true, I didn't want to be the one to stand between him and a child who wanted to be with him. When we were kids our Godfather, Uncle Billy, gave Jen and me a picture, which hung on the wall in our room until the day we packed up our deceased parents' belongings. Jen asked me if I would mind if she kept it and, of course, I didn't. It was a framed print of a throng of children gathered around a smiling Jesus, who is looking into one of the children's eyes as he gently cradles her face in his hands. Below, it read, "Let the children come to me ... The kingdom of Heaven belongs to such as these." Jen hung it in her hallway next to the portraits of her children. Before she died, she gave it to me and told me to take good care of it. I gave it to Lily for her room at the group home. The artist was able to convey a beautiful familiarity between the children and the man. When I was a kid, I would picture one of the little girls reaching up and playfully tugging on his whiskers. That would be Lily. If there is a Kingdom, Lily is most certainly a favored princess who could, not only get away with such antics, but actually make the King quite happy with her self-forgetting playfulness. The rest of us would be afraid of what he might do to us if we did more than curtsy. Lily has always seemed so at home with spiritual things. When she was a kid even, she was so peaceful at Mass, resting her head in someone's lap and stretching out on the pew if there was room. Every time I saw that, it would take me back to that moment when I decided the fate of my sister's children, and I would get this sense of something like pride welling up. I don't know, maybe not pride, but just a secure knowledge of having done the right thing by keeping them together. No matter the cost. And I don't think the cost could have been any higher.

One day, after we had returned from a family vacation to the beach, Jack embarked upon a topic that I had been trying to avoid for more than a year.

"What are we doing, Bev?" he asked.

"What are we doing?" I said.

"Yeah, I mean, is there something I'm missing here?" The vein in his left temple popped out, like it always did when he got agitated. "Is this the way life is supposed to be?"

"Is *what* the way life is supposed to be?" I dreaded asking.

"Miserable. I mean, are we supposed to be miserable all the time?" He ran his hands through his hair. "I mean, I know we must have been happy at one time, but I can't even tap into any of those feelings anymore. There's nothing here in this house but a dangerously high level of stress."

"That's not true," I yelled. I didn't want to sound indignant or defensive, but he was launching into ridiculous exaggerations. There were times of stress, but that wasn't the norm.

"What are you talking about? A dangerous amount of stress? You spend seven days with us, and you can't handle the little inconveniences that come with raising a family."

"*I* can't handle it? Like *you* can?" His eyebrows jumped quickly and fell back in place.

"How would you know about dangerous amounts of stress?" I said. "You're never home."

"I'm never home because I'd rather be at the office working than in this mad house," he flung his arm when he said it, like he was practicing his tennis backhand.

"Oh, yes, you've been at the office *working*." I'd had my suspicions for a long time, but I hadn't planned to outright accuse him. Not yet, anyway.

"Yes, I've been working," he said angrily. "What else would I be doing?"

"Hiding."

That was the end of that conversation. Neither one of us were ready to take it any further at the moment. So Jack went for a walk and I went to bed.

I remember reading an article one time in the early 2000s about how the installation of windmills in a rural area was ripping families apart. A 48-year-old New York man had refused to talk to his father, who had signed an agreement with the wind company to allow them to put seven windmills on the family farm, in exchange for $46,000 a year. The son was so annoyed by the noise and strobe effect of the turbines, that he nursed a grudge against the 95-year-old father fit for publication by CNN. I thought it so ridiculous, I decided to google windmill trauma and found other communities dealing with the same troubles.

"Our whole family has been affected," complained one woman. "My husband just went to the doctor because of his stomach. He hates those windmills. We have fights all the time about them. It's terrible. Why did you put them so close to our new home and expect us to live a normal life. If it isn't the shadows it's the damn noise."

Now I happen to know that these people's lives were not blissful until the windmill invasion. The father and son no doubt have a long history of battling over one thing or another. The windmills just give them something fresh and new to bicker about. The stomach troubles are probably from eating too much ranch-dipped chicken fingers and you can't tell me quarrelling with your husband is something new brought on by rotating blades. Solid families do not let the *whoosh, whoosh, whoosh* of turbines or the flickering shadows of alternative energy blow them apart.

This is how I came to understand what happened with me and Jack. I always said it was the stress of raising the children that led to the break up. But, really, how accurate is that? I lay there in the dark, my mind flying through the past three years, crash landing on a March morning in 2017. Lily had asked for a bagel for breakfast. The sign for bagel was the same as the sign for toast or any other kind of starch. It was the touching of her index finger to her thumb, other three fingers up, waving swiftly in the air. It was technically close to the true sign for French Fries -- an "F" bounced twice, but it had come to represent, to

Lily, anything that was not meat or vegetables. I proceeded to the kitchen and spread cream cheese on the bagel, trying to ignore the bad feeling in the pit of my stomach. The bagels that Jimmy and Terry had chosen from Einstein's that week happened to be green in celebration of St. Patrick's Day. I knew this was going to be a problem and I should have turned back right then. But I was hoping to prove a point, once and for all, that not all things green are to be loathed. Knowing how much Lily loved bagels, this was going to be my chance. Immediately upon seeing it, she recoiled in horror as if I had just served her roaches on the half shell. "Eeeeew," she screamed. I tried to convince her it tasted exactly the same as any normal bagel, but she would have nothing to do with it. I told her she wasn't going to get anything else to eat until she at least tried a bite of it. As the words left my mouth, I regretted them. You don't set up challenges like that with a child as stubborn as Lily, unless you are willing to devote an entire day to front-line combat. But once the gauntlet was thrown down, I couldn't back down. It's Parenting 101. You don't make empty threats. Say what you mean and mean what you say. Lily kept screaming at me throughout the day for different food. I didn't relent until 1:30, when Jack came home from golfing and shot me a look -- half of disdain and half of confusion -- not knowing, or not caring, that there was more at stake here than a piece of bread tinted a color not known to nature.

"Just give the child something she likes," he said through clenched teeth. "What's wrong with you? I wouldn't eat that damned thing either."

I said nothing and I made Lily a box of Kraft macaroni and cheese. She sat there, shoveling it into her mouth, until she had eaten the whole thing. Meanwhile, my resentment ate at me.

****

When Jack came back from his walk, I pretended to be asleep. He plopped down on the bed, hard enough to wake me if I had been sleeping. There was something he needed to say, and it couldn't wait until morning. He switched on the light to talk to my back.

"Bev?" His voice was low and stern.

"You're giving up on us, aren't you, Jack?" I said, without moving.

"There's no 'us,' anymore, Bev. There's you. There's me. There's you and the kids. There's me and the kids. But there's no "us." There hasn't been an "us" for a very long time."

I decided to make it easy for him. I didn't even turn toward him. "So, you've fallen in love with someone else, and you and she are going to go off and live in first person plural together."

Raising a child with special needs can act like cement or dynamite. We could have built something sturdy and strong, but instead it all blew up in our faces. We were good together as long as neither one of us needed to sacrifice, which we didn't as long as we only had to please ourselves for all those many years. Anything that would force us to put someone else's needs before our own would try us as human beings, including our role as spouses.

Jack was the one who did the cheating and the leaving, so he's the one who gets the blame -- on paper at least. But it wasn't entirely his fault. I was so wrapped up in taking care of the kids, I wasn't paying Jack much attention. But someone else was. The breakup of my marriage was another thing I secretly blamed my sister for. Her reckless decisions cost me my husband. I ended up a single parent when all I ever wanted to be was a childless wife.

When I think back over the timing of Jack's departure, it is clear to me what had become clear to him in that 10-by-12-foot hotel room with wall-to-wall, dawn-to-dusk chaos. Let's see, how difficult could his decision have been? On the one hand, there was us. One burned-out, irritable wife with menopausal hormone imbalance plus three argumentative, whiney, mopey, exhausted, elated, spastic children whose criteria for a good meal was anything that comes in a wrapper that you can wad up and use for target practice on your sibling's butt. On the other hand, there was her. A peaceable, well-rested divorcee who had nothing to do in her spare time but accessorize her designer clothing, cook her lover's favorite gourmet dishes, serve them up by candlelight and rub his neck by the fire he builds after dinner. I'm sure the decision became increasingly easy each time hotel management called our room to tell us fellow guests were complaining about the noise. It certainly wasn't the sort of noise Jack and his lover would have been making in a hotel room.

It occurred to me as the children stood barefoot in the wet driveway, watching Jack's brand new red Mustang coast away through the drizzle, that any marriage might have crumbled as a result of the misfortune that had befallen Jack and me. And then, for unknown reasons, as the tail lights on Jack's ridiculous emblem of virility rounded the corner out of sight, I thought of Lily's father and wondered where he was, if he had married and if that marriage had weathered whatever catastrophe life might have sent it. I felt certain I knew the answer. Thanks to my compliance with my bull-headed sister's deathbed coercion, that man had escaped the trials that had tested Jack and me and found our union wanting. And yet, I could not be happy for Lily's father. He had not known Lily, and that is quite an unenviable position. Now his daughter, too, is in an unfortunate predicament. She has no one but a dying old lady, whom she will not have for much longer. To this day, I rue the promise I made to my sister. Could there be a loophole in a promise like that? Now would be the time to find one, if one does exist. For Lily's sake, now would be the time.

7

CROOKED LIDS

After Terry and Jimmy went off to college, they stopped going to church and so did I. By then, Lily had gotten quite involved in the youth group and people from church were giving her rides to teen Masses, prayer meetings and potlucks and surprising her with holy cards and saints' medals on feast days. After high school, she got involved in the young adult ministry. People in that group, which was for singles, had a high likelihood of marrying each other. Lily is one of the longest-standing members. I know she has always dreamed of getting married, and I still don't think it's out of the question. She has had a few boyfriends who have Down Syndrome. I can't tell you how many times she has asked me "Mama, do you think I ever find a husband?" Now the standard answer my mother gave me when I asked that question had been passed down in our family for a number of generations -- from mother to daughter.

"Bev," my Mom said, rubbing a soapy sponge over the rose-colored Formica, "My Mama always used to say 'There ain't a pot so crooked that there ain't a lid somewhere to fit it.'"

Now this was somehow meant to instill a sense of hope in a young woman. But I took it as confirmation that I am a crooked pot, and indeed during my adolescence and even into my 20's I did seek out crooked lids. None of them fit, despite the fact that I tried on more than my share. So when Lily came to me wonder-

66

ing if she was worthy to be loved, I decided to break the chain of generations of trashed self esteems and put the crooked pot theory to rest right then and there.

"If some man is lucky enough," I said. A huge smile crept across her face and she squeezed me hard around my waist. That is one of Lily's greatest faults, if you can call it that. She hugs very hard. Terry and Jimmy call her The Mighty Python. The nurses here have all fallen victim to her embrace at one time or another. Maria gets a Lily hug every time she's on shift. That would be today, but Lily hasn't arrived yet.

"What are you eating today, Bev?" Maria asks, picking up my menu card. "Oh, you didn't fill it in yet. Do you want some help?"

"Oh, I didn't, Maria? I'm sorry."

"That's OK." She pulled a pen out of her pocket and bent over my shoulder with the card, pointing the pen at my choices. "Do you want the rosemary chicken or the Salisbury steak?"

"Chicken please."

"Mashed potatoes or rice?"

"Rice sounds good." Actually nothing sounds good, but rice does not sound awful.

"What kind of dressing on your salad?" Maria asks.

"Ranch on the side, please."

I watch her put "on the side" in parentheses. Her handwriting looks like the font they used to spell "Princess" on all the young girls' T-shirts, lunch boxes and notebooks when Lily was little -- sparkly pink accessories embellished with a rhinestone tiara over the word. It is appropriate handwriting for Maria. She looks like a movie character who has not yet discovered she is royalty. She wears no make-up, that I can tell, except maybe a touch of lipstick. I can never decide if that lovely coral is the natural color of her lips or not. It is obvious someone has invested a great deal of time in her. She seems well-cared for and meticulously taught -- manners, compassion, penmanship. I picture her mother spending Saturday afternoons with her, copying, "the quick brown fox jumps over the lazy dog," onto handwriting paper. I used to have beautiful penmanship when I was young, thanks to my mother, who had obsessive compulsive tendencies in almost all the right areas.

Before anything ever began to shake, I noticed my handwriting begin to go. The words were all cramped together and smaller than usual. Then one day, soon after that, I noticed my garage didn't smell like a garage any more. The smell of a garage is so identifiable, it transports me instantly to my grandma's house and makes me thirsty. Grandma used to let us go get Sprite or root beer out of the extra refrigerator in her garage and she would keep two red, ride-on tractors out there for us to use when we came to visit. The scent of garage is hard to describe, but maybe something like a delicious combination of rubber, slightly damp plywood, garden dirt and dust. I wondered what had changed in my own garage to rid it of that lovely link to childhood. Had the humidity dropped? Had I left the garage door open too long at some point, so that the fresh air had chased out the mustiness? A short time later, I realized that I couldn't smell the faint gas smell I used to when I first turned on my stove. And the Velvet Tuberose lotion that I once bought strictly because I loved the smell didn't have much of a fragrance any more. I also began to lose my appetite. Everything tasted like salty or sweet cardboard. I assumed I was suffering a bout of depression. Then, one day, on my 63rd birthday, I googled loss of smell and bad handwriting and was mortified by the possible diagnosis. These were the early symptoms of Parkinson's. Since I didn't have any of the shaking yet, I decided to try to put it out of my mind. Several months went by and one day my right pinky began to shake. I knew that was the beginning of the end. Not that I would die any time soon from the disease, but my life was ending just the same. I know people talk about different phases in their lives as chapters in a book. But this was not the end of a chapter. This was a book burning.

"Alright, Bev," Maria says, putting the menu card in her pocket, along with her pen. "You're all set. I'll get this order in. Would you like some clean sheets today?"

I like how Maria treats you like an equal. Some nurses pour on the saccharin in their zeal to show you how much they care, using a tone normally reserved for small children or companion animals or speaking to you in first-person plural: "How are we doing today?" I understand how easy it is to slip into that. I think maybe I have done it myself to fellow residents. Agnes and I are probably among the sharpest ones here. It would be nice if this disease would continue to spare my intellect. It often does. On the other hand, losing my mental capacity doesn't scare me as much as it should. I guess I've been around Lily long enough to understand that intelligence is not the key to happiness. In fact, it seems to me, it can be an obstacle. I remember one Christmas long ago that was particularly difficult. Jack had just moved out and we were neither in the money nor the mood to provide the kind of Christmas they had grown accustomed to. Terry and Jimmy were really down. The only time they said anything to me was when they could find a way to use me as an emotional dart board. "This turkey's a lot drier than last year." "Maybe next year we can get some *good* presents." "Lindsay is lucky she gets to spend Christmas with her Mom *and* Dad." "Can I go over to Zachary's house? They're playing football in the back yard all day." There they sat, slumped on the couch, feet propped on the coffee table, heads so heavy with disgust, they could barely hold them up. Meanwhile, Lily had discovered a treasure. A feather had poked its way through one of the throw pillows on the couch and Lily had managed to pull it out. She was laughing hysterically, blowing it into the air and trying to catch it as it came floating back down. Lily loved Jack as much as anybody. Maybe even more. But a feather had entered into her world at this moment in time, and feathers are funny things, whether you're living in a two-parent household or in a broken home with your deceased mother's sister.

There were moments like that which were so endearing that even a hard selfish old clod like me couldn't help but feel this sticky heaviness in my chest that I came to understand as attachment. One time I took the kids to the zoo and on the way out, I told them they could each choose something from the enormous toy shop. The older two picked some cheap noisy plastic animals with candy inside. Lily looked at everything in the store very carefully and decided on a new set of coloring pencils. She was only six. Every once in a while, you'd get a glimpse into her heart like that. You needed that glimpse because, since she couldn't talk for so many years, many things about her were a mystery. Like why she found it so harrowing to step off a curb, but she begged to go on the roller coaster at LegoLand seven times and still hadn't had her fill.

****

Although it didn't have the name Parkinson's until the early 1800's, symptoms of this hell I'm living were described in ancient India as early as 5000 B.C. It wasn't until after "An Essay on the Shaking Palsy" was published in 1817 that the disease was officially named after the author of that article, a London physician named James Parkinson, member of the Royal College of Surgeons. I rather like the sound of that. I mean, if you were going to have an organ removed, wouldn't you want one of those guys to do it? Hey, if they're good enough for the queen's gall bladder. Soon after I was diagnosed, I looked up Dr. Parkinson's essay online. Probably wasn't a good idea. Every once in a while, for reasons I cannot explain, I turn the audio on my Kindle and listen to it again. The description is at the same time poetic and horrific.

"The unhappy sufferer considers it as an evil, from the domination of which he has no prospect of escape."

More than 200 years later and there's still no prospect of escape. The royal surgeon goes on to describe the various stages of agony, which I have to say, from my experience, are highly accurate. It's a rare moment when something isn't shaking.

"Commencing, for instance in one arm, the wearisome agitation is borne until beyond sufferance, when by suddenly changing the posture it is for a time stopped in that limb, to commence, generally, in less than a minute in one of the legs, or in the arm of the other side. Harassed by this tormenting round,

*the patient has recourse to walking, a mode of exercise to which
the sufferers from this malady are in general partial."*

That used to be true for me, but these days, the muscles are
just too stiff, and I am mortified by the thought of finding myself
splayed out, nose-to-nose with whatever bacteria is growing on
these floors.

*"The propensity to lean forward becomes invincible, and
the patient is thereby forced to step on the toes and fore part of
the feet, whilst the upper part of the body is thrown so far forward as to render it difficult to avoid falling on the face. In this
stage, the sleep becomes much disturbed. The tremulous motion
of the limbs occurs during sleep, and augment until they awaken
the patient, and frequently with much agitation and alarm."*

I often have to trick myself to sleep. One of my techniques
is to close my eyes and visualize an image of Monet's water li-
lies, shrunk to the size of a postage stamp. The painting is the
one that has the clouds reflected in the water where the lily pads
grow. One of Lily's therapists gave her a poster print of it when
she had heart surgery -- I assume because of her name -- and it
hung in her bedroom until the day we moved out. I'm not exactly sure why it works as a sleep aid, but I guess the energy it
takes for my brain to project an image on my eyelids exhausts
me. To be successful, I have to keep the image on, even though
it wants to flash on and off. Often, the picture floats through the
past, guiding my mind to a place I've been long ago. Last night
it floated through the aisles of the Asian supermarket, where
Jack and I used to shop after taking a Thai cooking course. Past
the pig snouts, cow tongues, processed squid, lemon grass standing tall in black buckets of water, Thai eggplant, dusty cans of
coconut milk, bamboo rice steamers and colorful plastic toy dra-
gons that play *It's a Small World After All.* Sometimes the
postage stamp floats through the future, leading me through everything I will be doing the next day. Why my brain wants to go
through five or six dress rehearsals for simple tasks like brushing
my teeth and buttoning my shirt I will never understand. Some
people say they get to sleep by thinking of nothingness -- just
black space. But I was never skilled at making my mind do that.

Before I came up with the postage stamp trick, I would lay awake at night for three hours or more. And that was on non-chattering nights.

My jaw tremor acts up when my mouth is at rest, so talking and chewing gum provide the only relief. Can't do that in my sleep though. The chattering seems so much faster than what might happen to your jaw if you're cold or anxious -- like about 200 clinks per minute. It's near impossible to sleep through all that noise inside your own head. Then, every once in a while my jaw will snap shut so hard, I don't know why my teeth haven't shattered right out of my head. Wouldn't surprise me if they did, considering how bad they've gotten. It's been a long time since I could brush them well myself.

Lily has done the best she can to brush my teeth for me, but she doesn't have the world's best coordination either. Some of the nurses do a nice job. Others seem keen to the fact that they'll collect the same paycheck whether I have tartar build-up or not.

"The submission of the limbs to the directions of the will can hardly ever be obtained in the performance of the most ordinary offices of life. The fingers cannot be disposed of in the proposed directions, and applied with certainty to any proposed point .... Whilst at meals the fork not being duly directed frequently fails to raise the morsel from the plate: which, when seized, is with much difficulty conveyed to the mouth. The power of conveying the food to the mouth is at length so much impeded that he is obliged to consent to be fed by others."

A well-behaved tongue is a very easy thing to take for granted. Mine might as well not even be a part of me, for I have no control over it. I'm not talking metaphorically now, because you know I've never been a diplomat. I'm talking anatomically. There are some days when it's like having a trembling fish in my mouth. It ceases to perform any of its intended tasks, like pushing food to the back of my mouth and helping me swallow. By the time Lily is through feeding me, she has gone through five or six paper napkins, trying to keep my chin clean. I try to order foods from the menu that aren't too messy. I can't taste anything

72

anyway, so I might as well skip the chocolate cake. I never thought there would come a day when not even a seven-layer slice of heaven would give me pleasure.

When Lily was little, I never gave her a choice of ice cream. It was vanilla or nothing because I knew it was going to be drooled out onto her clothes, and vanilla doesn't stain. Eventually, she became a skilled enough communicator to ask for chocolate. I would lie and tell her there was none left after everyone else got some. She'd get mad, but I'd set the bowl of vanilla in front of her and after a brief protest, during which she would turn her entire body around in her chair and refuse to look at it, she relented and picked up the spoon. If I had it to do over again, I'd invest in a bottle of Spray & Wash.

I know I should probably feel embarrassed that Lily has to wipe the drool off my face, but I wiped hers so often, I guess I figure its pay-back time. A variety of different business establishments have this uncontrollable desire to give children lollipops -- the hair stylist, the banker, the doctor. I used to dread those places. Lily could liquefy an entire lollipop in her mouth without swallowing a drop of it. The goo would drip down her chin, mingle wildly with her shoulder-length hair and I would end up with a miniature version of the bearded lady and a mess so involved that it practically required a haz-mat crew to clean up. Because cleaning up afterward was such an intensive process, I used to try to hide the lollipops from the kids. It was easy enough at the bank drive-through because I would just take them from the tube that is sucked in and out of the teller window and sneak them into my purse. Then I'd eat them after everyone went to bed. One time I wasn't covert enough and Terry caught a glimpse of three suckers being shoved into my purse.

"Auntie, can I have the yellow one?" she blurted out.

I shot her a look. "Shhh."

"What?" she whined. "Why can't we have one?"

I sighed heavily and passed three of them back. "Give one to everyone," I said.

Lily kicked her feet and said, "yay!" when Terry handed her the red one. Jimmy and Terry both hated cherry-flavored candy.

Terry used to say red candy gave her a sore throat, but I think she was just associating it with cold medicine. Jimmy took the green one and I waited for a protest about why Terry got to choose first, but none came.

Three minutes later, I looked in the rear-view mirror and Lily's chin looked like a candy apple. Knowing it would be ridiculous and bordering on cruel to get angry at a child with low facial muscle tone for doing something as benign as enjoying a sweet, I hurled my frustrations at Terry.

"Look at her," I said talking to the rear view mirror. "Will you just look at your sister, Terry. You're going to be cleaning her up. I'm tired of it."

"OK, Auntie," she said humbly. "I'll clean her up as soon as we get home."

"You're the one who had to have the lollipops," I continued, trying to justify my rant. "So you're the one who's going to clean up the mess."

"OK, Auntie," she confirmed. "Lily, do you want to take a bath when we get home?"

"No," Lily said.

Of course, any other time, she would have begged to take a bath. But because it appeared someone else wanted her to, she was going to say no.

Jimmy just sat there making snapping noises with his mouth, alternately licking and looking at his lollipop.

****

I guess there are certain advantages to being debilitated at this time in history. With no technology -- no TV, no kindles, no computers, no audio books -- Dr. Parkinson's patients had nothing to do to pass the time. It's mind boggling, though, that for all the marvels of modern-day medicine, they still haven't come up with a cure, or even a way to effectively treat Parkinson's. In the beginning stages, the medication helped and probably gave me several more good years, where I was almost symptom free. But eventually, the effectiveness of the medication wore off and actually caused worse symptoms than the disease.

Walking was often my only relief from the all-over body tremors. But it didn't come easy. Every time I got into a crowd, my feet would refuse to rise off the ground. The only way I could walk was to scuff my feet across the floor. I would think of those old clips of Tim Conway on the Carol Burnett Show I used to watch as a child. I used to laugh so hard at that old man with the spiky white hair and baggy trousers. I now realize the poor character probably had Parkinson's. He walked in that ridiculously amusing way because he was afraid of falling on his face. Normal walking requires one foot to be off the ground at any given time. With both feet on the ground the chances of falling diminish. Your brain saves your body by refusing to let it lift its feet. The only thing I couldn't figure out is why, in the beginning, my feet only shuffled when I was in a crowd. Then I realized, it had to do with the oblivious passers-by, who had no idea how scary their frenetic pace and unpredictable darting is to someone whose only goal is to stay vertical. I remember once a feeble old man flashed Lily a terrible scowl for having waddled into his path. I never forgot his ire. I always assumed he disliked her because she was disabled. I now realize, he was probably envisioning the floor coming up to greet his nose because a chubby, careless little kid wasn't watching where she was going.

Dr. Parkinson's description about what ultimately happens to his name-sake's victims terrorizes me, but I make the Kindle read it to me anyway.

"As the disease proceeds towards its last stage, the trunk is almost permanently bowed, the muscular power is more decidedly diminished, and the tremulous agitation becomes violent ... His words are now scarcely intelligible ... The saliva fails of being directed to the back part of the (mouth), and hence is continually draining from the mouth, mixed with the particles of food, which he is no longer able to clear from the inside of the mouth ... As the debility increases and the influence of the will over the muscles fades away, the tremulous agitation becomes

more vehement. It now seldom leaves him for a moment; but even when exhausted nature seizes a small portion of sleep, the motion becomes so violent as not only to shake the bed-hangings, but even the floor and sashes of the room. The chin is now almost immovably bent down upon the sternum. The slops with which he is attempted to be fed, with the saliva, are continually trickling from the mouth. The power of articulation is lost. The urine and feces are passed involuntarily; and at the last, constant sleepiness, with slight delirium, and other marks of extreme exhaustion, announce the wished-for release."

The wished-for release. I'm sorry to admit, I have thought of sneaking the butter knife off my dinner tray and hiding it under my mattress. Or saving up my pain medication and taking it all at one time. The depression of this thing is unbearable, not to mention the physical torment. I was so pleased when euthanasia finally became legal in the 20's, but Parkinson's does not qualify as a terminal illness, so the mercy killing laws don't apply. They wouldn't apply to me anyway, because I'm more scared of what might happen to Lily if I die than what will happen to me if I live. I don't know how much longer I have, but it frightens me to think what she's going to do when her job here is done. What if no one ever really needs her again? Agnes says she will look out for her and ask her to come visit. I hate to ask Terry or Jimmy to take Lily on. Their families have crises of their own. Plus, Lily would have to move states, leaving everything and everyone she's accustomed to -- her job at the grocery store, her group home. I have fantasies of finding Lily's father in a nursing home and transferring him to this one. Lily's life could go on status quo, minus me, plus him. Nobody needs to tell me the odds of that, but an old woman should be allowed her wishful musings.

As difficult as it is thinking about a child living without you, it beats the alternative by a wide margin. Losing her has always been one of my greatest fears, and to tell the truth, maybe one of the biggest obstacles in letting myself love her long ago.

One time, I had taken Lily to a park while we waited for Terry and Jimmy to finish soccer practice. I noticed a woman there watching her. She seemed mesmerized watching Lily tag the other children with her smiley little growl. Since Lily was the slowest, where ever she went, she was chronically "it." Most children hate being "it," for more than a minute or two. It gets old having people run away from you. Lily didn't mind. Her appreciation for the thrill of the chase made her very popular on the playground. When the "one-two-three, not it" countdown ruled out all other "its" but Lily, a big smile would creep across her face and she would take off running and screaming and the kids would scatter in laughter. But usually, because Lily lacked a certain amount of coordination, she would take a spill at some point. Which is exactly what happened this day. The woman who was keeping a wistful watch on Lily must have noticed that she belonged to me after I made my way over to comfort her. As I returned to the park bench, the woman ambled closer and with a smile said, "I have a special girl, too. She's in Heaven now."

"Oh, I'm sorry," I said. "How old was she?"

"She was five. She died of Leukemia."

"Oh, I'm very sorry."

"Thank you." Lily let out a loud roar and captured the woman's attention again. "She is so cute."

"Thank you," I said. "What was your daughter's name?"

"Her name is Jennifer."

"That's my sister's name," I said. "She died of cancer too. Actually, Lily is her child."

"Oh, so you're raising her for your sister." This seemed to please her.

"Umm hmm."

"God bless you," she said, putting her hand on my arm. She had a large cluster of small diamonds on her front finger. "I know it's hard, but she'll give you more than you'll ever be able to give her."

Jen had told me that Lily needed to be checked for Leukemia every year. I had her blood tested just after her seventh birthday and she was now almost 9.

"How did you find out she had Leukemia?" I asked.

"She would get these bruises that just wouldn't heal," the woman said.

I wondered if that was happening to Lily and I just hadn't noticed. No, I thought. She rarely ever gets bruises.

"I miss her so much," the woman said. Her eyes -- encircled with what I imagined was dark, sleepless grief -- were fixed back on Lily now. "She was very special. But it does my heart good to watch your daughter. She's an angel."

I imagined that little girl's casket, white, set in the foreground before her weeping mother's face, which suddenly morphed into mine. The odds of Lily dying young have always been higher than most. Having Down Syndrome had put her at risk for all kinds of other ailments that could take her early: thyroid problems, high blood pressure in the lungs, childhood Leukemia. We're still dealing with her heart condition and sleep apnea and the increased risk of Alzheimer's Disease. And there was something else. A mother feels her child's pain in multiples of ten. If I were to become her mother, it meant I would have to suffer with her. And all her life, there will be dreams she never will fulfill. What of driving a car? Getting married? Buying a house? Having children? I knew there would be children who would tease her, adults who would never understand her and love interests who ignore her. And I soon came to learn there would even be savages who want to see her dead.

I always knew people could be cruel, but I could never have been prepared for the depravity of the comments I saw on You-Tube while doing research on Down Syndrome. Someone had posted a video of a relative with Down Syndrome playing air guitar while listening to his I-Pod. The man looked about 20 and was a bit spastic in his attempts to keep the beat, but he was having the time of his life, enjoying the attention he was getting from the camera. I scrolled down to read the comments and was horrified. Until that moment, I had no idea the caliber of hatred Lily might encounter in her life. The language was so disgustingly repugnant, I cannot bring myself to repeat it. But just imagine the ugliest thing that can possibly be said about a human being, and you haven't even come close.

The most disturbing thing about stumbling upon those vile comments is that it was like looking into a fun house mirror. I saw some of my own beliefs reflected back at me -- distorted and hideously exaggerated, yes -- but still recognizable as my very own. I remember the first time I ever gave any thought to the idea that people's lives did not all have the same value. There was a story in the paper in the early 2000's, a couple of years before Lily was born, about a man who jumped into a septic tank to save his son, who had fallen in when the lid gave way. The father of seven grown boys was an athletic director for a private college, obviously a very intelligent and accomplished man. His 20-year-old son had Down Syndrome. The father was able to hold the son's head above the sewage until help came to pull him out. But the father -- and grandfather to 24 -- drowned. I thought to myself "what a waste of such a gifted and productive life, just to save someone who would probably contribute very little to the world and die young anyway." I was ashamed of the thought and briskly chased it from my head, only to have it return throughout my life in a number of distressing disguises.

Now comes a dawning in my gut, a possibility I have not considered until this moment. What if Lily's father had exhibited some level of inexplicable disgust for her differentness? Could that have been the reason Jen wanted him erased from Lily's future? That would explain the adamant resolve of a woman who had behaved otherwise reasonably and rationally in most every aspect of her life. Maybe my promise is best kept after all. There has to be a lower-risk method of finding Lily someone to love.

8

MONKEY TOES

I usually try to be dressed and sitting when Lily comes to visit because I don't want her to worry. Plus, she typically goes to work right away on my hair. But on this particular day, I don't know if it was the new medication or a chemical imbalance, or just the release of pent up sorrow that had been stored over the decades in a reservoir of tears. But it must have been a shock for Lily to come in and find me lying in bed sobbing.

"Mommy, what wrong?" She held my head in her lap and stroked my hair. "Tell me what the matter."

"It's nothing, Honey."

"Please, Mommy. Tell me."

I struggle to lift my head and bring my hand to my face so I can wipe my wet cheeks. "I'm OK," I say.

I don't know what to tell her. There are so many things that are the matter. In fact, I can't think of one thing that isn't all wrong. This place, this body, this mind, the past, the future, the here and now. It is all so horrible. And nothing about any of it is ever going to change. Not for the better anyway. Tears have never come easily for me. I've always envied people who can have a good cry. Like Jack. We used to go to movies and he'd be sniffing and wiping his eyes with the knuckles of his forefinger, and I'd be sitting there fully absorbed in the plot thinking "how sad." I'd end up nauseated, but not in tears. My stomach takes the brunt of my heartaches. How I've avoided ulcers all my life I'll never know.

"Do you muscle hurt?" Lily asks.

"No, no."

"Do you wan- me to rub you back?"

"That's OK," I say. "Can you just pass me another tissue?"

She gives me the box. "Hey, do you wanna watch Gilligan Island? I think it on."

"Yeah, yeah," I say, blowing my nose. "That would be good."

As I watch the Professor try to cure the Skipper's amnesia through hypnosis, I wish that I could be struck with memory loss. I wish I could forget everything except who Lily is. I miss Terry and Jimmy. I miss Jen. I even miss Jack.

I want to have just one more conversation with Jen. Maybe she was right, and there is a Heaven, and I will be able to tell her all the things I was wrong about. That probably doesn't sound much like Heaven to most people, but there is one thing in particular I need to talk to her about. I want to get down on my knees, put the back of her hand to my forehead and weep. If it wasn't for Jen, I would be completely alone right now. If there is such a thing as angels, I have inherited one. I did nothing to deserve her. I said everything I could to destroy her. And yet, here she is, washing my face with a warm cloth while her favorite show plays behind her. She doesn't know -- and never will -- how much I didn't want her. She is so full of goodness, she could never comprehend that kind of inhumanity. I wish I could do something to make up for it. I wish I had the opportunity to rush into a burning building to save her. Or give her my lungs or something.

On this night, Lily doesn't try to trick me into eating. She just sets down the fork when I say no thank you. Then she walks the tray down the hall, as she always does, to the nurses' station where all the plates with half-eaten dinner rolls, untouched domes of mashed potatoes, wadded napkins smeared with fuchsia lipstick and flexi-straw wrappers are piled on a rolling cart.

Lily returns to my room with a large grin and two sticks of cinnamon Trident. She has a gum supplier at the nurses' station and she's on shift this evening.

"For after I brush your teeth," she says, with the same enthusiasm as if she'd just procured a $299 bottle of Astralis wine, vintage 2003.

"Oh, Lily," I say, "you never forget my teeth, do you, Love?"

"You know what they say," she says. "Ignore your teeth and they go away."

Lily tells that joke nearly every day. I read it on a poster at our dentist's office when she was about 12 and I drew her attention to it. She thought it was the funniest thing.

Lily routes around the bathroom drawer for my toothbrush and the Crest without looking. She's smiling at herself in the mirror. She has done that ever since I've known her. She has always loved cute -- dolls, real babies, puppies. Her own face.

"OK, open up," she says, still screwing the cap back on the toothpaste.

"You remember, Lily, when you used to give me such terrible fits about brushing your teeth?" She scrubs away at my molars and gives me a cup to rinse and spit. "You would chomp down on the toothbrush so hard, I couldn't budge it to save my life."

"I'm sorry, Mama," she says, but her sheepish smile tells me she isn't. "I let you brush them now." She holds the toothbrush out to me and opens her mouth wide.

"Oh, Lily, that's gross." I grab the toothbrush from her and toss it back in the drawer.

I always marveled at Lily's sense of humor. There's a level of sophistication about it that blind sides me just about every time I witness it. But she always did love to laugh. I knew early on that Lily was sharp in her own way because she understood irony. One time, when she was about nine, I was reading her one of her favorite Curious George books. The mother duck was followed by four yellow baby ducks. Lily was going through a phase where she named everything after her family members. She pointed to the first duck and called it Terry, the second was Jimmy, the third was Lily. So I said, "And what about this little fellow. Is that Sunset?" She burst out laughing. "No, that a duck, not a cat!" she exclaimed. She saw no problem with humans being ducklings, but a cat couldn't be a duck.

****

I watch Maria stretch the compression sock over my foot, swollen like a bratwurst. She folds it like an accordion and inches it up my leg. I search her face for signs of struggle, but there are none. She is my favorite nurse, by far. Always maintains a sweet smile while taking care of her patients, and in their moments of agony, her eyes, locked on theirs, reflect a small part of their suffering. She wears an oval medal close to her neck. I know it is a saint medal of some sort, but I can't see well enough to make out any detail. I sometimes want to ask her about it, but I don't want to open up any doors to a theological discussion.

"OK, Bev, how does that feel?" she asks, looking up into my eyes, my foot still resting in her lap.

"Fine, Honey. Fine."

"Good," she says, patting the top of my foot gently. "Let's get the other one on."

As she lifts my other foot onto her lap, I see a much older hand clenched around a much smaller foot. My mind is back to a Sunday when Lily was six. Terry had been begging all week to go to church and I was a little perturbed that I had to get everybody ready. It was a muggy summer morning. I was having hot flashes and I resented having to wear pantyhose on a weekend. Now I can't imagine a foot less convenient than Lily's. It was wide and short and the front toe was spread way apart from the rest, as if there was a sixth toe missing in between. Her physical therapist used to call them tree-climbing toes. And they would have worked fine for that, but she was not a monkey, and therefore had to wear shoes to church. The problem was, whenever you try to slide a sock onto such a foot, the big toe catches in it, adding an extra 15 or 20 seconds to the process. And on this particular day, that small thing seemed like a big issue to me. As I went to put her shoe on, it became apparent, after all that struggling with the sock, that I hadn't been successful in getting the sock in place and it started to bunch up inside the shoe. I knew that would mean trouble, since Lily hated that feeling. So I decided to avert a disaster and take the shoe off and try to straighten the sock. Well, that sock was stretched onto her chubby foot so tight, that in trying to get a grip on it, my index fingernail snapped. Without even knowing I was going to say it, I muttered under my breath, "I hate getting you ready." After I said it, I wished I hadn't, but I took momentary comfort in the thought that she probably wouldn't notice or really understand what I had said. As I struggled to get her shoe back on, I looked up and saw tears in her eyes. Her bottom lip was pushed out as she stared down at the ground.

"I'm sorry, Lily," I said, kissing her. "I'm sorry. I love you."

From that moment forward, whenever I helped her get dressed, Lily kissed me on the top of the head or grabbed my hand and planted a kiss on it.

Maria gently squeezes my foot, and the gray, bland present takes possession once again of my thoughts.

"OK, all set," she says. "Do you need anything else right now, Bev?"

"Oh, Maria," I say, shaking my head. "I don't know where you get your patience."

She puts her arm on my shoulder. Her medal dangles gracefully with the angle of her body. "It's easy with people like you," she says.

People like you. Not all the nurses would refer to us as that way. There have been times when I've been wiped so hard, I know the person wiping has no inkling that there is a human being inside this soiled skin. And I know there were times when I did the same to Lily. The stress of the entire day would converge like a vortex over her and let loose its force on what I saw was her refusal to take time to use the toilet. I can just imagine what she saw as she looked into my face, twisted with disgust at her inability to do what all normal children can do. I can imagine it because I've seen it on a number of faces here. Maria, on the other hand, seems to understand the dignity of a human being, even an incontinent one.

"My grandchildren are coming to visit," I tell her as she wraps the blood pressure cuff around my arm.

"Oh, really?" she smiles. "When?"

"This summer."

We're both quiet while she listens to the beat of my pulse. Then she lets the air out of the cuff and says, "I didn't know you had grandchildren."

"These are Terry's kids," I say. "She's bringing her family out for summer vacation." Terry and I need to talk about Lily's future -- what's going to happen after I pass on.

"Oh, how nice." Maria says, unwrapping the cuff. "How old are they?"

"Nine, 11 and 14. I have two more too. My son Jimmy's kids. They're six and four." I'm not sure whether to mention the one on the way.

"Well, I can't wait to meet them," she says, writing on my chart. "I have a two-year-old nephew, and I just adore him. He's my big brother's baby."

"I never thought Jimmy would ever settle down," I say. "He liked to travel and have fun with his friends. And the girls too, I think. But I guess he found one that was too irresistible." My voice sounds garbled and faint inside my own ears and I wonder if Maria knows what I'm saying.

"That happens."

"He's a wonderful father."

"Oh, that's great." She picks up the small potted plant on my night stand. "Do you want me to give this plant some water?"

"Sure, thank you." I try to wipe a stray strand of hair off my forehead, but my trembling hand keeps missing. "You're not married?"

"No." Maria wipes away the hair for me before she takes the plant to the sink. Her hand feels soft and warm on my forehead. She looks to be in her mid-20's, but she has an uncommon wisdom about her. Her face is fresh and flawless, like someone who's never even been glanced at by evil. "It's hard to find the right person these days. I guess I'm pretty choosy."

"Well, you can afford to be," I say. "You're such a lovely girl, with such a good heart. We can sense that, and we appreciate it. We don't always get treated so well."

"Oh, I'm sorry." She folds a paper towel and places it on the fake wood night stand to catch the possible drips from the plant. "You should always be treated well."

"Well, we patients aren't always a bed of roses either," I say. "I can't tell you how often things come out of my mouth and I'm listening to myself say them and thinking, 'Is that really me acting this way?'"

"Well, it's understandable when you're in pain," she says. Her eyelashes are the longest and straightest I've ever seen. "I hope I will have as much grace under fire as I see around here."

She reaches behind me to adjust my pillows. Her medal is almost close enough for me to make out some detail. I would have guessed the patron saint of nurses or somebody like that, but it looks like a man.

"Do you need anything else, Bev?"

I don't, but I dread being alone, so I figure I'll keep the conversation going and if it gets too heavy, I'll just tell her I'm tired.

"Who's on your medal?" I ask.

Maria grasps it between her first finger and thumb and smiles. "Oh, it's St. John Paul II the Great."

"Oh, I remember him," I say. "You're too young, but I remember him well."

"He had Parkinson's."

"Uhuh," I say. "It was a big deal when he died. Millions and millions of people came to the funeral. I watched it on TV. There were people from all walks of life there. All religions."

"I heard somewhere, and I don't know if it's true, that he was the first pope in history to allow himself to be photographed while ill," she says.

"Really?"

"Yeah, I guess he wanted to show that suffering and dying is part of life. Just another step in the journey towards heaven."

The journey? I never considered myself on any kind of journey. My life felt more like an un-journey, like there was absolutely no destination and if there ever was, I had already arrived some time ago at this mire of stagnant misery. But if Maria is right, and I really am on a journey, my passport has long ago expired.

"And why are you wearing his medal?" I ask.

"Well, you might think it sounds a bit crazy, but I pretty much talk to him all day long," she says.

"Talk to him about what?"

"My patients," she says, nonchalantly. "I ask him to intercede for them. To help them."

Coming from anyone else, it would have sounded crazy. But Maria is the kind of soul that can make you think something as beautiful as that could really be true.

"Oh, Honey, I wish I had that kind of faith," I say.

She smiles and fixes my pillow once more. "You rest now, OK? I've got to go check on Richard and Lisa."

The next day, Maria tells me she downloaded something for me on my audio Kindle. It's an old *New York Times* article about John Paul II's beatification. Since I watched the news every day before the kids came to live with me, I had a vague memory of the story. I remember it had something to do with handwriting and a French nun.

I listen to the kindle quoting excerpts of the nun's testimony in which she describes how she was being ravaged by Parkinson's Disease to the point of being unable to write. The month after John Paul II died, the nun's congregation began to pray to the pope, because he had also suffered from the disease. One day, the mother superior asked the nun to write John Paul II's name on a piece of paper, but the name was illegible. The nun retired to her room that night and felt compelled to pick up a pen again. This time, the writing was clear. The next morning, she awoke without pain and attended Mass. Upon emerging from the church, she was convinced she was cured. A neurologist who had been treating her for some four years concurred.

I go to close the kindle and notice an envelope stuck in the inside pocket of the cover. I open it and find a John Paul II medal. I smile at Maria's goodness and feel a little guilty that she probably assumes I'm a fellow believer, based on my Mass attendance and the statue of Mary that sits on my shelf, complements of my Lily.

I let Lily rope me into going to the Mass offered here every week. It's the easiest way for her to get to Church, and I don't mind going. I've always told people I lost my faith in college. Because I had moved away from home, my parents were no longer in charge of making sure I got to Mass. I just33 found it dull and unnecessary to set my alarm on Sunday morning after partying so late on Saturday night. That excuse, however, does not take into account Saturday evening Masses or even the one that was offered on campus as late as 9 p.m. Sunday. The real reason was the church's teachings did not support my view of morality. I saw nothing wrong with premarital sex and didn't want to remain intellectually dishonest by attending a church that did. I had friends who didn't have that problem. They would do whatever they felt like doing with whomever they felt like doing it on Saturday night and wind up in the Communion line on Sunday. I guess I'm simpler than that. I don't like being conflicted. I didn't want the church to tell me I was losing my salvation, so I opted to believe there is no salvation. It's just that now that death is so close, I'm not sure I like that theory so much anymore. Worst case scenario, I'm wasting an hour a week going to Mass. I've got nothing but time and nothing but misery to fill it, except the time I spend with Lily.

Sometimes when those automatic doors of the Manor House lobby open and Lily comes waddling through with her big smile, it hits me. One change in any variable and I would have nobody. If Jen had never met Lily's father. If Jen had taken all the advice about her pregnancy. If Jen had married Lily's father. If Lily's father had fought for custody. If Lily's father were to walk through that door right now and whisk her away. Most of these "ifs" nauseate me. That last one scares me to death.

9

COLLISION WITH DESTINY

Before Jen died, she gave each of her children a Bible. To Jimmy she gave the one she received on her Confirmation. To Terry, she gave the one Mom gave her when she left home, inscribed in Mom's beautiful script, "We're so proud of you, Jen. Always stay close to Jesus." To Lily she gave the Children's Bible that was given to Jen by our godparents when she was a baby. And she gave me the one she actually used, apparently on a regular basis. It had passages highlighted in yellow and pages that were accidentally creased. She had written comments and notes to herself in the margins. This I didn't know until years later because I had kept it packed in a box of items she gave me just before she died. One day, when I was having a particularly bad day with the kids and I was really missing the carefree days of my childhood, I wanted to remember what it was like to have a sister. I opened the box. Stuck between two pages of the 10th chapter of Luke was a print-out of an Erma Bombeck column, in which the humorist asserts that God very carefully handpicks those who will be the mothers of children with special needs, judging them good candidates if they are independent and have a working knowledge of how to laugh. And when the angel asks God which patron saint to put in charge of the mother who is to receive the child with disabilities, God tells the angel that a mirror will do.

I remember a snickering scoff escaping my lips as I folded the column and returned it to its place between the pages, where it has remained ever since. All I saw when I looked in the mirror was a map of wrinkles, deep ones charted by misery, minor ones by frustration -- all of a place I had no intention of ever going.

Also in the box Jen had bequeathed me was a photo of our family at the beach. Jen and I were quite small, maybe 4 and 6. We squinted into the sun with the corners of our mouths up-turned, but not quite smiling. We were both wearing the same thing -- yellow and magenta stripes on a one-piece swimsuit. Sand stuck to parts of us so it appeared we had been dipped in butter, rolled in sugar and baked. My right arm and Jen's left leg, my left cheek and her nose. I remember how even behind the white vinyl shower curtain back at the cold hotel room, the sun-tan lotion and sand mixture weathered the warm water as well as you'd expect from a quality stucco.

The next thing I unpacked from the box was a senior high school year book. Jen was two years behind me in school and as I thumbed through the pages, I recognized quite a few kids, ei-ther because they had siblings my age or Jen was a friend of theirs. The most flamboyant signature was from Simon Bonfig-lio, a boy in her grade who had a crush on me. He penned his page-long epic next to a shadowy black-and-white photo of him-self playing oboe in the jazz band. He covered everything from the boring chem teacher to spilling spaghetti on somebody's shirt and ended it with the directive, "Tell that foxy sister of yours I said 'hi' and that Franklin High is not the same without her." Next I pulled from the box a small clear plastic container with a dried-up rose, brown around the pedal's edges with no hint of what color it used to be. It was our Dad's wedding cor-sage. I wondered why Mom gave it to Jen instead of me. Maybe she hoped it would bring her some sort of luck in finding a mate.

At the bottom of the box was an unfinished manuscript of a novel Jen had been writing. The sticky note on top said, "Dear Bev, feel free to finish this up for me. Love Always, Jen." As much as I love to read, I've never written anything in my life aside from what I'm "writing" now. I always thought I'd have time to write after the kids grew up. Now I've got this Parkinson's, which I can't honestly use as an excuse, since all I would have to do is dictate it to my hand-held. I know it would be a great story if I could ever get it done. It's a romance novel, but a sophisticated one. I was thinking maybe I'd have Agnes help me finish it sometime.

In her book proposal, Jen says she invented the story one day in the lobby of the hospital, where she was receiving chemo. I wondered why she would start a book after being diagnosed with cancer. A book is not a short-term project. She must have had hope for survival. Or maybe just wishful thinking. I know, for myself now, how comforting it is to have a project you have to work on tomorrow. Now I know why so many old folks crochet very large afghans. Since I can't do that, I try to get the longest audio books I can find, Like *Les Miserables* and *War and Peace*. Novels I shied away from when I was younger because the task just looked too daunting from the vantage point of page 3. Now I realize I should have read them when I was young. I would have had a better chance of finishing them.

I lifted the cover letter to my sister's book and read the summary.

A young, attractive doctor, working in a hospital, tolerates an endless parade of suitors -- usually well-off doctors, who talk almost exclusively about themselves, except for brief interludes when they would marvel at the odds of someone like her existing. Someone beautiful, who also has the intelligence and the drive to enter their noble profession. From this information alone, they had gleaned that she would be a suitable mate for themselves and mother for their children, or at the very least, a very interesting distraction from the stress of saving lives. Beyond what they could have learned from a photo and a resume, none of these men knew her. Despite always having a dinner companion, she was a lonely soul. At least when you're by yourself, you can think your own thoughts, find memories and day dreams to keep you company. But being with someone who is disinterested is desolation. Self-absorbed people absorb more than just themselves. They sop the joy from your insides, leaving a dry, achy kind of loneliness.

The doctors would always take her to upscale, trendy restaurants, where the waiters wore crisply ironed white cotton shirts and spoke of everything in first-person possessive. "My soup tonight is a pumpkin cream with duck confit. I also have some special entrees that are not on the menu. I have a tender ox tail over pan-fired polenta served with stewed lentils in a black currant gastrique. Also, tonight for you, I can offer my braised rabbit in a tangle of pappardelle with mustard and tarragon crème fraiche. I hope you'll try to save room for desert, because I have for you this evening a delicious whole roasted fig with goat cheese ice cream and oatmeal tuiles, which goes beautifully with a glass of my collioure wine."

Let me get this straight, she wanted to say. The chef spent four years in culinary school and another 15 experimenting with flavors and presentations, the farmer planted and harvested the ingredients, the truck driver drove them across the country, the restaurant owner took out a loan, signed a lease, hired an interior designer and took out ads in the local paper to get me here to eat it, the sous chef and his crew chopped, sautéed, seasoned and plated it. You, then, picked it up from the kitchen and carried it to the table. And it's your dish.

The hospital where Dr. Robyn Stanich has worked for the last thirteen weeks is set up like a big square donut. The second, third and fourth floors are open in the middle so you can look down to the first and see the grand piano that sits in the lobby. There is one time of day when that dry ache inside her subsides, giving way to a soft euphoria. It is when that sweet and complex music wafts up into the third floor ICU. The janitor takes a break from his duties every evening at 6 p.m. and plays the Bechstein. Some evenings, Dr. Stanich will stand in the hallway and look down. The janitor's dust mop is propped against the piano, and he is pouring his entire soul onto the keys. One time he looked up, for no reason at all, except that he must have felt someone's eyes on him. He caught her watching him and a little smile. Then he returned to his passion. She had never heard music like that before. She had never seen a man like him before. She wanted to know him. She wanted to fall in love with him.

But there were problems with that idea. He was below her, not just by two floors, but in just about every other way as well, she surmised. He was probably about eight years her junior. He was obviously not a professional. He was most probably not as educated. He probably had very little money. Maybe even lived in a trailer. None of this really mattered to her on an emotional level, but she knew the odds of such a thing working out were slim. He wouldn't understand her career, her drive, her long hours. He'd resent her for making more money than he did. Plus, the entire hospital staff would accuse her of slumming it and dole out slaps of snide congratulations on his back.

To heck with it. She wanted to fall in love with him anyway. She ached to love a man like him.

The following evening, he glanced up at the third floor to see if she was watching. She was. Her elbows were propped casually on the railing and she gave him a one-sided smile. He smiled back -- with his entire mouth -- and though he was a good thirty feet below her, she felt his eyes burn right into hers. She couldn't even tell what color they were from up there, but she knew at that moment a love affair had begun.

Even as old as I am, reading that made me want to fall in love. I can still remember the first time I saw Jack. It wasn't a romantic encounter by any stretch of the imagination, but I still felt like I was in a fairy tale. He was the insurance adjuster who handled my case after I was involved in a fender bender with an exterminator whose truck was retrofitted with bug antennas. We would always tell people we owe our relationship to a giant roach. Jack wasn't the traditionally handsome type. He was on the short side, a bit soft around the middle, but he had a tranquil smile and I immediately trusted him completely. I had never dated anyone I had trusted completely. Within the first fifteen minutes of filling out forms and answering questions written in dull legalese, I knew that I would say yes to him if he asked me out. In the next fifteen minutes, I began to send out vibes encouraging him to do so.

"I wonder how long it's going to take to get my car fixed," I told him. "I guess I'll be staying home for a while."

"Can't your boyfriend drive you around," he asked.

"Don't have one," I lamented.

"Oh, what a pity," he smiled slyly. "Well, there's always public transit."

He let several seconds go by as he looked down at his paperwork, feigning disinterest. "Or, uh, I could always give you a lift. Like to dinner or the movies."

"That's OK," I said, coolly. "I'll catch a bus."

"Pretty girls like you shouldn't ride buses," he said.

"Oh, really?" I said. "I haven't heard that one."

"Well, it's true," he said, raising one eyebrow. "It's really quite risky. See, you'll get on at Union Street, and there'll be no more seats left, and Prince Charming will give you his, and before you know it, wedding bells will be ringing."

"And that would be bad because..." Fill-in-the-blank, Mr. Greeley.

"Because, for the rest of your life, you'll sit in your castle and ponder what might have been between you and that dumpy-looking, yet strangely magnetizing, insurance guy."

I laughed and stood to leave. "You've got my number," I said motioning to the file, lying open on his desk.

"How are you getting home," he asked.

"The bus, of course," I told him. "You just better hope Prince Charming's trusty steed is not in the shop."

One thing Jack and I had an abundance of was humor. At least in the early years. Somewhere along the line, I stopped laughing at his jokes and sometime thereafter, he stopped cracking them. I began to worry about our marriage when Jack spent a majority of his words reminiscing. At first I thought he was just trying to share his past with the kids. But trips down memory lane became almost an obsession with him. Literally. Every time we'd drive by his old street, he'd tell the same stories. There was the Seven-Eleven where he'd stop to buy a Slurpee and a Ding Dong after school. There was the house of the girl that gave him his first kiss. There's the park where he met his best friend. He talked about it with such fondness that I knew he wished he was back there -- away from us. It was the same thing with music. He started to download all the music from when he was young, wishing the clock backwards. All of this I could not relate to at all. I didn't have a bad childhood, by any stretch of the imagination, but my fond memories were extremely limited. Jack used to talk about how great it was to be a kid and not have to worry about anything. I worried about everything when I was a kid. And still do, I guess.

Jack would have loved his funeral. His two brothers and sister talked a lot about his childhood. They apparently loved it too. A typical number of tears were shed at Jack's funeral, which was seven years ago now. But only one person wept, and that was Lily. She loved Jack so. His second wife sniffed into pink tissues and dabbed at her eyes. She looked pale and too exhausted to cry anymore. Her children sat one on each side of her and held her up. It looked like a Kennedy moment. Lily said after the funeral that they never should have dressed Jack in his pin-striped suit. He looked too uncomfortable. She said she wanted to be buried in her purple flannel pajamas. I thought that made a lot of sense until I pictured how odd it would be to wear your pajamas in public, especially when you're the guest of honor and all eyes are on you. Lily sort of saw my point and then said maybe jeans and a sweatshirt would be better. Regardless what she wears, I know Lily will definitely want to take at least one purse with her into eternity. When she was a kid, she would emerge from her room everyday with about seven purses hanging on her. She had stuffed them with all her belongings, with no particular order that I could ever determine. One purse, for instance, would have a lego piece, a doll's baby bottle, a hair band, a shoe string, a paper clip and a broken crayon. Another would have a doll bootie, a Barbie hat, a hair brush, a Polly Pockets doll, a bandana, a cotton ball and a price tag off a recently-purchased article of clothing. It was as if she were trying to cover her bases in case she happened to run into Monty Hall. And it typically broke down like this: a third of the stuff she'd taken from Terry's room, a third from Jimmy and a third was her own.

Thankfully, Lily ended her career as a thief once she finally started making and spending her own money. The concept of personal property began to sink in and she shifted her obsession from thieving to giving. One month, she ended up spending the entirety of her salary on stuff for her friends and family. She stayed after work scouring the aisles for what she considered appropriate tokens of affection and gratitude. She gave me, for instance, a party-sized bag of Ruffles, a large silicon spatula, a 12-pack of Three Musketeers bars, a 36-count package of clothes pins, a pack of AAA batteries, a four-pack of cigarette lighters, a 3-pound bag of Granny Smiths, a double-decker bus matchbox car and a six-pound sirloin tip roast. I had to sit her down and explain budgets. We suggested she limit her gift giving to one small token per paycheck. Ever since then, she has purchased the same two items every payday: a pack of Freedent spearmint for me and a bar of Irish Spring for her father. The gum is easily consumable, but at last count Lily has accumulated 375 bars of soap in a 35-gallon Rubbermaid storage box used by most people for camping gear and sporting equipment. I've tried to convince her she probably doesn't need to buy any more. I will try once more today.

"I have to buy presents for Daddy," she insists, "Cuz I miss him. Soon I see him. I give him all the soap. From my heart. He gonna like it. The man on TV, he like it. He look jus- like my Daddy. So handsome."

She covers her sheepish grin with both her hands. "He not wearing any clothes," she whispers, her eyes twinkling with impish delight. "On TV with no clothes. That so silly."

"Well, he would look even sillier wearing a tuxedo or a leisure suit or pajamas in the shower, wouldn't he?"

Lily bursts into hysterics, tipping her head back, placing her hands on her head. Then she freezes and lets her eyes wander to the walls.

"When I gonna see my Daddy?"

"I don't know, Lily. But one thing is for sure. If he is ever fortunate enough to have you in his life, he will be a very clean man."

"Uncle Jack always clean," she says. "He smell good. I miss Uncle Jack."

"Me too, Honey."

"Mommy, are you gonna die?"

"We're all going to die someday, Lily," I say.

"Like Uncle Jack. Like my other Mommy."

"Yes. It's part of life, Lily."

"But, you not die soon, right?"

"I don't think so," I say.

I think about how badly Jen felt that she had promised Jimmy she wouldn't die. I don't want to do that. But I don't want Lily to worry either. We are having this weighty discussion while Leah, the nurse who has come in to give me my night meds, counts pills in a paper cup.

"Five minutes, Lily love," Leah tells her. "Did you have fun today with your Mom?"

Lily wraps her arms around my middle. "Mommy, I don-wanna go home," she says.

"Why not?" I ask.

"I wanna stay with you." She puts her arms around my neck and lays her head on my chest. "Can I spend the night?"

"I wish you could, Doll, but that's against the rules," I say.

Lily looks at the nurse. "Can I just stay a little longer?"

"You'll miss your bus," the nurse says kindly. "You don't want to do that, do you?"

"I catch the next bus," Lily says.

"But then you'll be here way past visiting hours," Leah says, "and someone will think you're an employee and we'll have to put you to work scrubbing floors."

"I don- mind," says Lily in a tone that every parent hears at least twenty-two times a day. "Please, can I stay?"

She is still talking to the nurse, but I think I better intervene to give the poor woman a break. I know how persistent Lily can be.

"You better go now, Lily," I say. "It will be way too late when you get home if you stay any longer. That might not be so safe. Besides, I'm getting very sleepy." I reached over and squeezed her in tight to me. "I'll see you tomorrow, OK?"

Lily has tears in her eyes. "OK, Mommy." She picks up her back pack. You be here tomorrow, right?"

"Of course, Lily," I say. "Where else would I go?"

She smiles.

"Love you, Lily." I blow her a kiss from my trembling hand.

10

PROMISES IN TURBULENCE

It is still dark in the room when I feel a hand on my shoulder.

"Mrs. Greeley, wake up, Mrs. Greeley. I need to tell you something."

Another voice comes, hushed and urgent. "Trina, no, don't wake her. We'll tell her in the morning."

"No, this can't wait," the other voice counters. I blink my eyes, which seem to have snap-shut hinges.

"I don't know if we can even get a van at this hour," says the farther voice.

"What's going on?" I sit up and try to focus on the nurse closest to me. I see the silhouette of the other against the harsh hallway light.

"Mrs. Greeley." I feel a hand touching mine. "There's been an accident. Lily is in the hospital."

"What? What kind of an accident?" I ask. "Is she alright?"

"It was a traffic accident," the nurse says.

"No, you must have the wrong person," I lie back down and close my eyes. "Lily doesn't drive."

"Mrs. Greeley, she was hit by a bus."

I jump up so fast, my head feels disconnected from my neck. "Is she alright? Where is she?"

"We're trying to get you a van, so you can go meet her at the ER."

"Please, please hurry." I struggle to get my feet to the floor. "Please, help me get dressed."

"OK, Mrs. Greeley. It's OK," she puts a hand on each of my arms. "We're going to get you to see your daughter."

"Trina, you might as well wait and see if we can get the van," the other nurse says.

"Get the van," I shout. "Please. I'm the only family Lily has. You've got to get the van." My normally faint voice booms inside my head.

When I arrive at the hospital, a doctor greets me and asks if I am the only next of kin. I think he is hoping for someone to comfort me after the things he is about to tell me. Or maybe he is hoping for someone a bit sharper, who can grasp it all. I tell him my children are trying to get flights. He is a kind man, but speaks to me as if I were a child, apparently assuming my mind is as enfeebled as my body. He tells me of skull fractures, broken bones, bruises and brain injury. How much only time will tell. The next 24 hours are critical, he says. He warns me that it is going to be difficult to see my daughter, and that, in fact, it might not look like her at all. There has been a great deal of facial swelling. There are bandages and machines. I tell him I need to see her right away, that we have talked long enough. The doctor has adequately prepared me, but hearing about it and seeing it are two different things. If I were standing, I'm sure I would collapse at the sight of her. As it is, I feel the breath go out of me, like someone has punched me in the belly, and then comes a tingling in my hands and feet. The doctor is right. It doesn't look like Lily. For a moment, I try to convince myself it isn't. This is someone else's loved one, and Lily is safe at home in bed. I wheel myself closer and suddenly feel as if my neck muscles have completely disappeared, leaving my head dangling just before everything goes dark.

I awake with an oxygen mask on my face in the ER. Now that all my vitals are close enough to normal, the nurse tells me,

I will be transported back to the Manor House. She promises I can return in the morning, but I wonder where she got the authority to make such a vow. Lily's not going to regain consciousness tonight, she says, so there's no point in staying. I can do her the most good by resting, so I can be here for her in the days to come, the nurse tells me. She removes the oxygen mask from my face and helps me into my wheelchair.

I lay in the dark, back at the Manor House, tormented by the creaks and shimmies of my bed, which quiver in concert with my muscles until the blue-grey light of morning squeezes in around the heavy cerulean window curtains. I ring for the nurse to get me ready.

Agnes is sitting in her usual spot in the common area when the medic wheels me by her on the way to the van. "You're going to see our angel," she says, grabbing my arm. She puts her fist in my hand and drops something cold and heavy into my palm. "Take this with you." It is a red glass-bead rosary with a gold crucifix. "It was blessed by John Paul II. At the Vatican," Agnes says. "I was there in 1984."

I plan to stick the rosary into the outside pocket of my purse when I get into the van, but for some reason I never do. I press the beads against my palm and find it comforting, like the comfort some people find in biting their bottom lip.

The city looks strange out the van window. People moving from point A to point B. Down the sidewalks, crossing streets, getting in curbside cars, standing at bus stops, riding bikes. I have spent so much time sitting in a very small corner of life that I have forgotten I once belonged to such a great vastness. The world looks foreign now, like seeing a strange civilization for the first time. My emotions are spent. I can only take it all in with a blink-less stare. I draw a long breath at the thought of Terry and Jimmy waiting at their airports in Denver and Minneapolis/St. Paul. They are due in the afternoon. I hope the trip won't be too hard on Terry. She has hated to fly ever since our one and only family flight, the summer after Jen died. On the way back from Disney World, we hit a sudden bout of severe turbulence. All the passengers were screaming and the coffee and pillows were flying and Jack was saying "wheee, a roller coaster," to keep the children from being frightened as we plummeted to what the rest of us assumed was our fiery death. When it was over, Jimmy begged Jack to get the pilot to do it again. Lily repeated over and over again the sign for "more." Terry cried for the rest of the flight, wrapping her skinny fingers around the armrests until all the pink drained out of them. When we landed for a layover in St. Louis, Terry refused to get back on an airplane. She pleaded with us to find a Greyhound bus. We told her it would take days to get home on a bus, but she didn't care. She said she'd promised God that if he got her on the ground safely, she would never fly again. I told her I'm sure God understands that she made that promise when she was terribly scared and not thinking clearly. She told me it wasn't the first deal she had made with God. She said she had promised God not to fight with Jimmy if he would make her mother well again. Terry wasn't able to keep her end of the bargain for more than a few hours.

"Maybe God would have healed her if I would have been nicer to Jimmy," she told me as people squeezed by us with their rolling luggage and carry-ons.

"Oh, Terry," I said. "A lot of people feel guilty when their loved ones pass away, but there's no reason to. When someone dies it is out of everyone's control. Your mother's death is not in any way your fault. It was just her time to go."

"We have to go now," said Jimmy, tugging at my sleeve. "Look, they're closing the doors."

Jack swooped Terry up before she had time to think any further and gave her a big smile. "Come on, let's go watch an in-flight movie," he said.

Jimmy took Lily's hand and followed close behind.

I wish Jack could be there for Terry on her trip out here. If he were alive, he would have gone to get her. I know he would have.

****

The medic wheels my chair to Lily's bedside.

"A little closer please," I say. "Thank you. You can just wait outside for me please." He hesitates before leaving. I'm sure he has been briefed on what happened to me last night.

I press my forehead against Lily's arm. It is cold and clammy, and I want to adjust her blankets so her arms are covered, but I won't have the strength at this angle. Besides, there is an IV hooked to her other arm. Her face is slack with sluggish muscle tone, and coming from her mouth is a large plastic tube snaking to the ventilator on the other side of the bed. The machine, which looks more like a piece of office equipment than a device that keeps someone on this side of death's door, makes a rhythmic hissing sound, surrogate breaths for Lily's lungs.

"Hi Lily," I say softly. It feels strange talking to someone who can't hear me. But it is equally strange being in the room with Lily and saying nothing. I remember the beads pressing into my palm. "Agnes sent you something."

I lay the rosary across her chest and take her hand in mine. I hope for even the slightest movement. "She got it blessed by John Paul II. He was pope when I was young."

Out the third-story window a cloud looms like a giant cauliflower over the horizon. I put my forehead back on Lily's arm and close my eyes. Tears squeeze out past my eyelids. I feel like a paraplegic all alone in a dark cave. No amount of wishing it was yesterday, no amount of hoping Lily would wake up, nothing can change anything. The toughest part is that Lily isn't able to tell me, the way she always does when I worry, that everything is going to be OK. I wonder, what would she have done if she were me? I press my eyes against my sleeve to dry them. I press so hard, I see those strange lighted images, like television snow on the dark orange screen of my eyelids. I press hard again and see Lily's face, smiling at me, the way she did when she first noticed I had awakened after passing out. I realize how much I need Lily. Other people probably won't ever get that. I'm not sure, until this moment, that I really ever got it. I always knew she needed me. But I *really* need her.

I place my hand on one of the large beads of the rosary that lay across Lily.

"Our Father."

The words are uncomfortable, but the gold metal links that hold the glass beads together sound almost musical in the grasp of my trembling hands. My fingers move to the small beads.

"Hail Mary. Hail Mary. Hail Mary..."

When I get back to my room, Monique is gone. I wheel myself into the hallway and flag down the first nurse I can find. She tells me Monique passed away. I wheel myself back to my room and look at her bed. The room seems abandoned and wrong, even though Monique never said a word or moved a single finger outside the tiny space she inhabited under her blanket. I sit there and try to figure out why I miss her. I wonder if they would let Agnes move in. I wonder where Agnes is. I didn't see her in the dining room. I remember today is mall day. A shuttle was going to Pacific Place. Agnes is probably over at Barnes & Noble, sipping tea and working her way through a stack of delicious new books.

Terry calls me on my cell to tell me she and Jimmy had caught a taxi from the airport to the hospital and are now heading my way. I wait in the lobby, as close to the automatic doors as I can get without triggering them to open. Finally, after a time of watching no one come or go, a taxi pulls up. While Jimmy pays the driver, I wheel myself through the doors into the drizzle.

"Oh, Auntie," Terry drops her purse on the wet sidewalk by my wheelchair, throws her arms around me and sobs like a small child. My tears flow too. "Are you OK, Auntie?"

Terry and Jimmy have called me Auntie ever since they came to live with me. Before Jen died, I was Aunt Bev. They probably figured, intuitively, or maybe Jen prepared them before she died, that first names aren't intimate enough for the person who has chosen to give up her life for you.

"It's so good to see you," I say, putting both my trembling hands on Terry's arms. "Did you see Lilly?"

"Yes," she nods and wipes her cheeks and the dark rings under her eyes with both hands at once.

Jimmy politely squeezes in between us, takes my hand and kisses me on the top of the head. "You doing OK, Auntie?"

"Yes, I'm fine."

"You look so tired," Terry says, brushing a stray strand of hair off my cheek.

"Oh, it's so good to see you both," I say. "How are the kids?"

"Oh, they're great," says Terry.

"Ornery as ever," Jimmy says. "Let's get inside out of this rain." He pushes my chair toward the doors, which open to release a large puff of warmth onto our faces.

"How's Georgia, Jimmy," I ask. "Does she still have morning sickness?"

"Yep," he says. "And she's just really tired."

"Oh, I wish I could be there to help with the kids," I say.

"We're getting by OK, Auntie," Jimmy says.

"Can I get you anything?" Terry asks me.

"No, I'm fine," I say. "Would you mind if we went back to the hospital now?"

"Sure, we can do that," Jimmy says.

Actually, no. We can't. We can't because I have to get out of my chair to go to the bathroom before we leave. A wave of purple, green and blue splotches wash across my eyes as I watch my feet touch the grey linoleum, and then a black curtain falls. Next thing I know, I wake up in my bed, and everything in the room is tinged orange with the setting sun. I look for Terry and Jimmy and call their names a few times before Agnes wakes up. She has dosed off in her wheelchair waiting for me to awaken.

"It's OK, Bev," she says, struggling to wheel her chair next to me. She takes my hand. "Jimmy and Terry will be back. They just went over to look about Lily."

"Oh, drat it, Agnes," I say sitting up and wrestling my feet toward the floor. "This stinking blood pressure of mine."

"Now, Bev, you just wait a minute," Agnes cautions. "We'll ring for a nurse to help you get up." She grasps the call button hanging from my head board.

"Is Lily OK?" I ask her. "Did you hear?"

"I didn't hear anything, Honey."

"Where's my phone," I ask myself, routing in the bedside drawer for my purse. "I'm going to call Terry and Jimmy and tell them to come back and get me."

Nurse Nora, the one with the large neck and veins that pop out on her forearms, saunters into my room.

"What's going on, Mrs. Greeley," she says in a tone that is thoroughly bored.

"I need to get over to see Lily," I say.

"You need to rest Mrs. Greeley," she says unmoved. "Doctor's orders. Maybe tomorrow. You ain't going nowhere tonight."

"All of my children are over there," I say. "I've got to go."

"Sorry," she says, wrapping a blood pressure cuff around my arm. "No can do."

"Agnes," I say, handing her my purse. "Can you find my phone?"

"Who you calling?" asks the nurse.

"My children are visiting Lily," I say. "I'd like to get an update. Is that OK with you?"

"Go right ahead," she says. She let the air out of the cuff and dropped my arm.

"Thank you." I take the phone from Agnes, automatic dial Terry's cell and put the phone to my ear. "What's my blood pressure?"

The nurse looks up at me from the chart she is writing on with a raised eyebrow. She might as well have said, "You talking to *me*?"

"85 over 55."

That's not bad," I say, listening to the phone ring in my ear.

"It ain't good neither -- for someone who likes to pass out a lot. You're not going anywhere tonight, Mrs. Greeley. Like I already said. Better yet, like Dr. Smythe already said." She seems glad about it.

As she leaves, Terry answers. Lily has awoken and is asking for me. Agnes pieces two and two together from listening to my side of the conversation. She might jump out of her wheelchair and do a jig.

"You've got to come back and pick me up," I tell Terry. I don't tell her the medical staff has forbidden me to go. By the time she gets back here I will have it all taken care of. There haven't been many occasions in my life when I have put up a fight. Most things just never seem worth it. But the staff at the Manor House on this night had better not come between me and that door. They had all better stand back. Way back.

I decide to save time by requesting to see a doctor right away and also the nursing home social worker, Claudia Vasquez. It is her job to sort out these conflicts of interest. Their risk management policies against my maternal instincts.

"Mrs. Greeley, I'm not trying to be unreasonable," says Dr. Smythe, "but you could slip into a coma. Let's give the medication some time to work and keep an eye on you tonight and see where we're at in the morning."

"Look," I say, grabbing the doctor's forearm. "I'm going to be at a Level I trauma center. If I have any sudden health issues, I'm sure they can take care of it." Better than this incompetent staff, I want to add. But I hear my mother's voice: "You catch more flies with honey, than with vinegar, Dear."

"Mrs. Greeley, I think Dr. Smythe is more concerned about the trip to and from," Claudia Vasquez interjects. She is leaning against the door jam, arms relaxed and folded across her chest, one high-heeled red pump propped on the other, in a casual, "no-need-to-get-yourself-all-in-a-lather" pose.

"Doc, come on," I say releasing my grip on his arm and looking into his eyes. "Do you have children?"

"Yes."

"What if one of them was lying in intensive care, calling out for you, after having been hit by a bus?"

The doctor glances at Claudia and closes his eyes for a few second as he breathes in heavy through his nose. "OK, Mrs. Greeley. You win."

"Thank you, doctor." I want to pick up his hand and kiss it. Instead I grab it and squeeze it.

"But stay in your wheelchair." He says it like a sore loser.

I nod. "Of course. I will." What was I going to do, go sprinting through the hallways of Harborview Medical? Handsprings maybe?

Dr. Smythe stands up and, without expression, heads toward the door. I grab my purse and drop my cell phone inside.

"Mrs. Greeley," the doctor says. I turn to look at him. He and Claudia are standing together in the extra-wide door jam. "I hope Lily makes a speedy recovery."

"Yes, me too, Mrs. Greeley," says Claudia, smiling sweetly.

"Thank you," I say.

"Everyone around here misses her," says the doctor.

I nod and feel a tear sting the outer corner of my right eye.

On the way over, I think about what Lily might say when she sees me. She will probably smile and say "hi" and maybe reach her hand toward me. I can't wait to tell her how much everyone misses her. But things we anticipate rarely ever happen the way we think. By the time Terry and I get to the hospital, Lily is so exhausted, she has fallen back asleep again. Jimmy had stayed with her while Terry was picking me up. He says she had been awake until just about a half hour before I got there. The nurse says it is not uncommon for patients with head injuries to sleep for quite a while after waking up the first time. She advises that we just let her rest. I so needed to talk to her -- or really, to hear her talk. But it isn't going to be tonight. I just hold her hand and whisper to her "I'm so glad you're getting better, Baby."

Terry has brought a scrapbook of old photos for Lily to look at when she wakes up. She thought it might help with the recovery process to jog old memories. She and Jimmy and I thumb through the pages as we sit in Lily's hospital room, listening to the beeps and whirs of near-death technology. We find the page with Terry's wedding. I had almost forgotten what Jack looked like. He was terribly handsome in his tuxedo. We all looked darn good that day. I don't think Lily knew she could be so lovely. Terry had arranged to get all her five bride's maids' hair done. Imbedded in Lily's sweetheart curls were deep purple velvet ribbon bows to match her dress. All day, she would eye herself in mirrors, windows, anything the least bit reflective -- just like a little girl playing dress-up.

It was the first time the kids had seen Jack in more than a year. He hadn't sent for them that summer because he and his wife had taken a European vacation, and he said he'd just see them at the wedding. Lily spent as much time as she could -- pretty much whenever she found him seated -- sitting in Jack's lap. He doted on her and told her probably a hundred times how pretty she looked. "I'm gonna look even prettier when I'm the bride someday," she told him.

"I don't know how you can possibly look any prettier, my lovely Lily," he said, squeezing her tight and planting a kiss on her cheek.

"Terry look prettier cuz she wearing white," Lily said. Ever since that day, she has wanted to be a bride.

"Well, I'm partial to purple," said Jack.

"Maybe I carry pu-ple flowers then," she said.

"Do you have a fella picked out yet to marry?"

"No, no- yet," said Lily. "I looking for someone like you. Or my other Daddy."

That's a statement Terry never would have made. She was still mad at Jack for cheating. Lily never understood the details behind Jack's departure, nor did anyone try to educate her on it. She loved him so much, it was better that her love remain un-vexed. Jack had the decency to leave at home his Margot, whom he said was sick with the flu and couldn't come to the wedding. Strange to say about someone who cheated on you, but Jack always was a class act. I don't know why, I felt very little animosity toward him. Just a tinge of embarrassment. I think he felt it in my presence as well. It's as if we both failed at something.

Lily danced more than anyone at the reception. Jack, Jimmy and Terry's new husband, Jacob, saw to that, along with all the groomsmen. At one point, one of them even cut in on the other. Lily was glowing. I thought about how different this all could have been if Jen were here. She would have given a speech that would have brought everyone to tears, even the caterers who didn't know Terry and Jake from Eve and Adam. I would have been on the guest list as the adoring aunt, most likely arm-in-arm with Jack. I felt a strange emotion I can only describe as a close cousin of fear at the thought of that scenario. The what-if had momentarily robbed me of what I had come to treasure most. I literally shook my head to push it out of my mind. I watched my sister's three children, all grown up, move about the dance floor at the helm of a joyous commotion, reassuring myself that they were indeed mine. I raised my goblet, in a toast to thin air, just in case Jen had a way of looking down on all of this. If I had been a woman of faith, I might have felt a clink against my glass.

11

TV DEBRIS

Agnes is waiting up for me when I get back to the nursing home. She is in the lounge reading *Of Mice and Men*. It is just after 9:30. The steam rises from the Styrofoam cup in her hand, propped on the tartan green and blue plaid throw that is draped over her legs.

"Hiya, Bev," she says, laying her open book face down on the table next to her. "Did you get to talk to her?"

"No," I say. "She was back to sleep by the time I got there."

"Oh, that's too bad, Honey." She rubs the fringe of the throw between her thumb and forefinger. "How is she looking?"

"She looks OK, I guess. Doctors are happy with her signs of progress."

"Praise God."

"I really have to talk to her, Agnes," I say. "There are so many things I need to tell her."

"I know, Honey."

"I need to tell her I'm sorry."

Agnes nods. "There are always things we want to tell our loved ones sorry for," she says.

"There were just moments," I say. "There were times when I was not so patient."

"We all have those moments, Bev."

112

"Well, I had too many," I say. "Things weren't ever as serious as I made them out to be."

"Aw, that's all part of being a parent," she says, swatting at my guilt as if it were a fly. "Children know how to push your buttons. I never even knew I had so many buttons 'til I had kids." Agnes raised four.

I look around, and we are the only ones still up, except for a nurse behind the desk. "So what kind of tea you drinking?"

"Ceylon. Do you want some? My daughter sent me some new bags. I'll ask for some hot water for you."

"No, it's OK," I say. "I'm beat anyway. I should get to bed. I'm going over to the hospital first thing in the morning."

"OK, Hon," Agnes says winking. "It's a good idea to get some sleep."

I sit there for a minute, nose pointed toward the floor, analyzing the subtle zigzag pattern of the carpet. "You know, there's one thing I wish I could say sorry for, but I don't guess I ever can."

"Nonsense," Agnes says firmly. "You can always say you're sorry. The good Lord always hears you."

"I think He's the only one I should ever tell," I say. "It's something that would break Lily's heart."

Part of me wants Agnes to ask me details, but she isn't the type to probe. It's the part of me that wants to tell another living soul, so it can go on record somewhere in the history of man that I am so very sorry that I never wanted Lily, I mean in the beginning. And sometimes I wonder. Did I treat her that way -- like I didn't want her? I tried never to let on. But all those times when I rolled my eyes or drew a heavy sigh or raised my voice, did she understand that I saw her as a burden?

"Being a parent is tough," Agnes says. "I can't even imagine what it would be like having kids with special needs. I lost my cool plenty when I was raising my kids. You know, I always said, I thought I was a good person before I had kids. Then I realized just how selfish I was."

"It is eye-opening," I say.

"Eye opening?" she snickers. "It can make your eyeballs explode right out of their sockets. My grandkids, they don't believe their parents when they tell them stories of how I used to lose my temper. I didn't do it very often, but boy, when I did, look out. One time, I actually smashed a television in the middle of the living room floor."

"You didn't, Agnes." I chuckle at the thought of someone so frail and mild going on a rampage in front of her children. "Not you."

"Oh, well, you know how it is," she says, waving her hand disgustedly. "The kids were fighting again about what they were going to watch. So I decided to put a stop to that nonsense once and for all and bust the TV into a billion little bits." The b's explode off her lips like the low tones plucked from the strings of a classical guitar.

"Was that effective?" I ask.

"Well, it did stop the fight. For the moment. I still feel bad about it. I just thank God no one was hurt by the debris."

I just hope Lily was never hurt by my debris.

****

"Lily, hello Love," I say, getting my face as close to Lily's as I can. "I wish you would wake up. I really want to talk to you." Her face is blank and swollen, like it is fashioned out of grey dough with too much leaven. Her color makes it difficult to believe what the doctor's had said -- that she has made remarkable strides in the last 24 hours. They have taken her off the respirator. They are still giving her oxygen, but she is breathing on her own now.

"Mommy." Lily's eyes are still closed.

"I'm here, Baby," I tell her, squeezing her hand. "Are you OK?"

She turns her head toward me and opens her eyes.

I smile wide at her. "We all miss you so much." I kiss her hand. "You had an accident, you know. Do you remember, Baby?"

"No." Her voice is faint like mine. She tries to blink away her confusion.

"I'm so happy you're OK, Lily."

"Am I OK? I don- remember."

Yes, Love," I say, stroking her hair. "You're OK, and you're going to get better every day."

"OK," she says, closing her eyes as if she means to rest them for several minutes. But they immediately open again.

She lifts her arm slowly, and looks at the IV secured with three strips of white tape wrapped around her wrist. "This hurts. I wan- it off."

"After you start eating and drinking, the nurses will take it off," I say, lightly patting her arm.

"I eat some cheese," she says. I burst into tears at the realization that my Lily is back. She is truly back. Her old mouse-girl self. American cheese has always been, by far, her favorite food. I ring for a nurse.

"Are you hungry?" I ask, trying to steady my hands to wipe the tears off my cheeks.

"Yeah. I wan- some cheese."

"OK, Baby, the nurse is coming."

Suddenly, her eyes look far off, as if she is remembering something from twenty years ago. "Mommy," she says. "I saw my other Mommy."

"You saw her?"

"Yeah, I saw her in my heart," she says. "She smile at me and hold my hand."

"Oh, that's so nice, Lily," I say squeezing her hand. "I really miss your Mommy."

"Me too," she says.

"Do you remember Jimmy and Terry were here with you?" I ask. "They just went down to the cafeteria. They'll be right back."

"Terry and Jimmy," she smiles slightly. "Oh, yeah. They came to visit me."

"Yes, they did."

"Can they come over to my house?" she asks.

"Not today," I say smiling at the memory of a chubby 10-year-old in pony-tails, asking that question of grocery clerks and bus drivers and librarians -- anyone who would give her a smile and a kind word. "You have to stay in the hospital for a few days."

"Why?"

"You were hurt and now you have to regain your strength," I say, patting her hand. "The doctors and nurses are going to help you."

Then, Lily, for the first time since the last time she was with me at the nursing home, erupted into a full smile. "I *love* doctors, she says.

I imagine she might be referring to one, in particular. Even an old woman like me can't help but notice how beautiful he is. Very tall. Very brown, with deep Latin eyes and the thickest head of hair I've ever seen. Lily has always been fond of men. Any time we got together with other families, all the children would run off and play, but Lily would loiter in the living room with the adults, waiting for the other kids' father to notice her. After she'd successfully charmed him with her fat-cheeked smile, she'd grab his hand and lead him to the toy she wanted to play with. Then she'd sit down and pat the ground, inviting him to sit with her. If he took her up on it, she would be his shadow for the rest of the evening, calling him Daddy and manipulating him into being her personal playmate, until I'd shoo her away for the seventh or eighth time with my repetitious admonition that it's not polite to be a Daddy hog.

Although, sometimes it was quite useful. You know that feeling you get when you look in the rear view mirror and real-ize there's a cop back there. It's a multi-faceted emotion -- disbelief, fear, indignation, guilt and shame. Well, 6-year-old Lily must not have read any of that on my face, because she had only elation when the solemn-faced officer with a heavy dark mustache appeared at the window of our Dodge Caravan.

"Good morning, ma'am," he said in a robotic voice. "Driver's license, registration and insurance, please."

I dug into my purse. A wadded up tissue, a sanitary napkin and a lint-covered raisin tumbled out as I extracted my wallet.

"Do you know why I pulled you over?" he asks, not looking at me, but somewhere far off down the street.

"Uh, no, officer," I said, managing a polite smile as I stuffed everything that was not my wallet back into my purse, including, for some reason, the raisin. "I don't." I hoped it was something as benign a bad brake light.

"Do you know what the speed limit is at Neely?"

"Um, 40?" I stuck my fingers between the Macy's charge card and the grocery store membership to pinch out my license.

"No, it's 35. Do you travel this road often?"

"Every day to bring the kids to school," I said. "I guess I never noticed the speed limit."

He shook his head. His pen made scratching sounds on a yellow form attached to his clip board.

"Moms in mini-vans," he muttered. "They're the worst."

He took a second look into the back seat. In the rear-view mirror I could see Lily smile very big and wave. "Hi," she said.

"Hello," he managed a smile and waved back. "You going to school?"

"Yeah," she said.

"Where do you go to school?"

She just smiled.

"Are you in kindergarten?"

"Yeah," she said.

"You're a cutie," he said. "I have a little boy in kindergarten. He'd like you."

His gaze returned to me, but his jaw was not as tight now. "Do you know how fast you were going, ma'am?"

"Well, it must have been pretty fast if you pulled me over." My way of telling him that I knew he was in complete control of this situation.

"Not really," he said. "Forty-five."

Lily wanted to continue her conversation, and all this talk about speed limits was getting in the way. "Daddy, Daddy, Daddy," she was yelling from the back.

The officer looked at her. "Hi, Daddy," she said.

"Hello, Miss," said the officer. He lifted the yellow sheet and started writing on a white one. "I tell you what. Since you're such a nice girl, I'm going to give your Mommy a warning this time." He ripped off the underneath sheet and handed it to me, along with my documents. "Slow down, OK?"

"OK, officer, thank you. I will."

That day when I picked Lily up from school, I took her to get ice cream. Chocolate.

****

Love for a child hits you in the strangest way. It feels like something huge and molten inside your chest, a frothy concoction you might find churning in a candy factory vat. It comes on suddenly and for unexpected reasons. It happened once when Lily was little and eating a plate of lasagna I had made. She pierced the large slab of pasta with her fork and was gnawing pieces off. Despite the difficulties of negotiating such a large portion, she had refused to let me cut it. With her lips pushed out and her eyes closed, she looked something like a calf chewing. She was enjoying her food immensely. It was at that point that I caught sight of her enormous eye lashes. I wanted at that moment to throw myself in front of a locomotive to save her. Motherhood is bizarre. Why would I gladly and without a split-second's hesitation, run into a blazing building to rescue Lily, but resent having to get up off the couch to pour her a cup of milk?

Sometimes the day-to-day care of a child requires nothing short of heroic acts of virtue. I remember days when my back was so sore because Lily had refused to do anything she was supposed to and I had to physically lift her from place to place -- onto the toilet to pee, off the toilet to pull up her pants, onto the stool to wash her hands, off the stool to wipe her hands, over the threshold to give the next kid a turn in the bathroom, onto the chair to eat dinner, off the chair to go take a shower, into the shower, out of the shower, over the threshold again, into her room to find pajamas, into her bed to read a book. All the while the screaming protests that never worked, except to make me angry enough to finally explode into a very loud "BE QUIET and QUIT YELLING!" Which also never worked. She and I both engaged in the same ineffective repetitions over and over again, like rats in a maze, failing time and again to locate the cheese, but never altering their route. And I was supposedly the intelligent one.

Besides "be quiet," the next two most common words in our house were "hurry up." It is an intrinsically impolite phrase because it implies that someone isn't living up to your lack of patience. Still, it can be said in a nice way. But I rarely did. It's just that I never could figure out how on earth someone could be slow at absolutely everything. Even flipping a light switch. Lily would press too lightly and be looking up at the bulb, waiting for it to come on. Eventually she'd figure out that she needed to apply more pressure to the toggle. I guess all total, it took less than five seconds, but when you're living your life hoping for split-second responses, you feel like climbing the wall while you're waiting for the light to go on. Now, it's me driving my own self nuts. I want to yell at my hand sometimes, "hurry up," as it makes its way to the switch and attempts to steady itself enough to apply the required pressure to turn on or off the light. Why I care how much time it takes me, I don't know. I've got nothing but time now, much of which I spend sitting around, thinking about all the ways I failed Lily. Time and insight -- I've got both now. And yet, I realize, for all my faults, Lily changed me in ways I never thought possible. You know you have entered the ranks of true parenthood when you find yourself putting your hands on things you were never willing to touch before. I used to have trouble even looking at a roach and would never have guessed I would pick one up with my bare fingers. Not until one ended up in my child's mouth.

The things that were once noxious enough to warrant a call to haz-mat were now handled with a casual once over with the garden hose or vacuum cleaner. I remember one day, there was this horrible smell in the back yard where Lily was playing. I thought it was a gas leak or a dead gopher, so I ushered her inside and went to investigate. I couldn't find anything. When I went back inside, the smell had travelled into the hallway. I followed my nose to Lily's room, where she sat playing with her dolly. I sniffed around and found that the smell was coming from Lily. I checked her pants. Nothing. I smelled her hair. It was horrible. Her hands, noxious. I didn't know what she'd gotten into, but I marched her into the shower and scrubbed her down. Even after several soapings, she still had a faint smell of something dead. I asked her what she had played with and she kept making the same sound over and over again, but I couldn't make out the word she was saying. I went back outside for a more thorough investigation and found a broken egg shell on the far side of the yard. Yep. That was the smell. Under a nearby shrub was the rest and the worst of it. Lily had found a hard-boiled egg after an Easter egg hunt -- five months after. Instead of dropping the rotten egg and taking cover from the horrible stench that was released when she disturbed it, she decided it would be a good idea to get a plate, break open the egg, sprinkle it with sand and serve it to her dolly, who sat smiling at the fare under a Pacific blackberry bush. It wasn't much of a mystery that Baby Alive didn't recoil in horror at the smell, but how on earth could a human being have endured it?

****

It's been six days since Lily regained consciousness. Jimmy flew home a few days ago, and Terry left yesterday. Lily is recovering well and I am able to go see her twice a week. My doctor doesn't want me making the trip any more than that, because of the physical strain. Terry and I spent the time Lily was asleep talking about long-range plans. And so, some thirty years later, after Lily changed my life forever, I find myself in my poor sister's shoes. I am now the one who has to beg someone to take care of Lily. I know what I'm asking, but I am truly a beggar. I have no one else to ask. Jimmy is sweet to her, but his children are still young and with another one on the way, and whatever that brings with it, I don't want to do that to his family. Terry said she and Jake would think about what to do. She and I talked about a number of options, including Lily coming to live with her. I hate that Lily would have to move and leave everything she has here. But I also hate the idea of her being without family nearby. Time and distance have done nothing to diminish Lily's attachment to Terry and Jimmy. With Lily, it's not like just any old warm body will do. Like her biological mother, she is accepting of all people of goodwill, but she chooses to bond with few. And although Lily's been hung up on seeing her father, even if he is alive and I was willing and able to find him, he ultimately may prove unworthy of her deep affections.

But whoever gets Lily won't have to cook another day in their lives. Ever since she was six years old, Lily has loved to watch the Food Network. She would sit in front of the TV and say "mmmm," "mmmmm," as the celebrity chefs prepared and plated up their specialties. On occasion, she would get so excited about a dish, she would jump up and down, pointing at the television, as if she were watching her best friend win Olympic gold. Every day, after school, she'd get out all her play dishes, her Fisher Price stove and colorful IKEA knives and park herself in front of Mario Batali or Rachael Ray. She would hold the ketchup bottle high over her saucer-sized frying pan and say "E.V.O.O." I never could figure out why Rachael Ray abbreviated that, when in the next breath, she always said "that's

Extra Virgin Olive Oil." Aren't abbreviations meant to save you from having to waste your breath on the long version? But I'm glad Rachael did abbreviate, because I know, at the age of six, Lily would never have been able to say, "Extra Virgin Olive Oil," but she was able to manage E.V.O.O. By the time she was 10, Lily had watched so many cooking shows, she could have probably landed a job at Berkshire's The Fat Duck, had chef Heston Blumenthal been willing to include on his upmarket menu a selection of plastic food served on pink pearlescent Barbie plates.

As she grew, Lily transitioned to real food and became quite proficient in the kitchen. Her specialty is rice pudding. She actually makes a better one than I do, and I haven't figured out exactly why, since I'm the one who taught her. Maybe it's because stirring is her favorite activity next to swimming and watching TV. She really has quite the patience for it, tending to her pot of pudding like a nursing mother. I'd always lose interest, walk away and forget to stir it. Then I'd spend half an hour scouring black pudding off the bottom of the pan. Lily was kind enough to me to use the Food Network euphemism and call it "over-caramelized."

I always assumed Lily talked to herself while she cooked because that's what she saw the television chef's doing. But one day I realized she does it with other tasks too. Come to find out, it's common practice among people with Down Syndrome. They are actually thinking out loud in order to stay on task, and if the rest of us weren't so worried about what other people might think, we'd all be doing it too. I've tried it, and it's actually quite helpful. My grandmother used to say you're not crazy if you talk to yourself, only if you answer. Well, now I know better, because Lily does answer. Actually, sometimes she and herself have quite a row.

One day I remember I had told her she couldn't go to the mall with her friends because she hadn't finished her homework. She went into her room, slammed the door and this is what I heard from the other side:

"I wanna go to the mall!"
"You finish homework."
"I don't want to. I want my friends."
"You obey mother."
"But I wanna go to the mall."
"Finish homework. Then go to the mall."
"OK. I do it fast."

Although I was glad when Lily learned to talk and was finally able to put an end to all the screaming over unfulfilled wishes, it took some getting used to her emerging role as narrator of her own life. The whole world now had access to the contents of her mind. It was interesting to see that, like most people with limited mental capacity, Lily had developed some very creative survival skills.

"Stir. Stir. Stir. Take pan off stove. Turn stove off. Check stove again." While she's saying, she's doing, in play-by-play rhythm, with a cadence that tells you she really enjoys the sequence she has mastered. She's in a groove. And a groove means it's going to get done right. And no house fires will result.

In addition to a dependable supply of delicious rice pudding, another advantage of living with Lily is your house will always be tidy. Lily is a creature of order. All things must be restored. So if you leave a kitchen cabinet open, she will close it. If you leave the lid off, she will replace it. If you leave the flap open, she will refasten it. Never you mind that you're still getting stuff out, it will drive her nuts until it's closed. She's been like that ever since I knew her. This, I believe, is a survival mechanism for people with slower intellects. If they didn't follow certain routines, they would end up eventually forgetting to do something important, like turn off the iron or let the cat in before the blizzard. When Lily was small, each night before she could sleep, she would insist on restoring her room to its original state. For a borrower like Lily, that meant ridding her room of everything that wasn't hers. Right after I tucked her in, she would get up again and take everything she had taken from everyone else's rooms all day long and place it in the hallway outside her door.

Then again, I suppose that all could have been a delay tactic to put off bedtime by a minute or two.

If Lily wasn't in the mood to go to sleep, she would do anything she could to thwart the bedtime routine. She would refuse to take a drink of water because she knew that's what everyone did before bed. For some reason, children turn into camels at bedtime. One time, Lily refused to go to the bathroom before bed, and I knew she hadn't gone in hours and that if I didn't convince her to go, I'd be cleaning up her bed in the middle of the night. I set her on the toilet, but you know what they say about leading a horse to water. It's true for the other end, too. She just sat there on the toilet and screamed at me. Moments like that were infuriating, but also encouraging. It meant her brain was scheming, and schemes require intelligence.

There came a day when Lily became petrified of the dark. We never figured out why. She would immediately get up after I tucked her into bed, as soon as I was out of sight, and turn on her light. I used to come back through and turn it off, right before I went to bed, usually about three or four hours later, when I thought she was in a deep sleep. Half the time, Lily instantly awoke and stumbled bleary-eyed to the light switch to turn it back on. I always wondered if she had transparent eye-lids.

Not only did she herself not want to spend a split second in a room without the light on, but she also went into near hysterics if anyone else turned out the light in a room she was not even in. This appeared so irrational to me that I'm afraid I wasn't very understanding. I would tell her, "Hey, knock it off. Get over it and go find something to do." Jack finally had to explain to me that Lily saw darkness as dangerous and that she was afraid for her siblings to enter it.

Jack had a sixth sense for Lily logic. For instance, there were certain places Lily just refused to step. One of them was the mat where we kept the cat food and water. If there was someone standing in the kitchen and the only route around them was across the cat mat, she would push herself against that person as tightly as she could, so as not to let her toes so much as

124

graze the mat. Jack theorized that she must have stepped on it at some point when water or cat food had been slopped onto it. Knowing how much she hated anything wet or cold on her feet, that made sense.

She also would not step in a stripe of sunlight streaming onto the floor of the open garage in the morning as I loaded kids in the car to drive them to school. There were many occasions that, upon arriving at school, I'd notice she had black smudges on her rear-end from squeezing herself up against the car to avoid stepping on the sun. Why did I even bother to wash clothes?

That, Jack figured, was because she had probably once stepped on cement made hot from the sun and wasn't about to get her toes burned again.

There were so many phases. One day, Lily just decided she'd been kissed enough for one lifetime. If you kissed her cheek, she wiped it off and said, "yuck," minus the ending "k" sound. She wanted to be the one to kiss you. She'd grab your face, turn your head to the side and smash her face against your cheek. If you tried to return the kiss, she'd wipe it off and start the process for planting one on you all over again. I don't know for how long this could have continued, because I always gave up before she did. I always assumed it was because she didn't want anyone's slobber on her. But one day Terry was making a Playmobil Daddy talk to her, and all of a sudden he kissed her. She wiped his kiss off too, and I know he didn't slobber.

I think what surprised me about Lily, even from the very beginning, was how logical she was most of the time. She actually seemed to have more common sense, at times, than Terry and Jimmy. Common sense is one of those things you often have to learn to live without when you're raising children. You always want to ask "why," or "What were you thinking?" But even if your children could possibly give you an answer, which nine times out of 10 they cannot, you don't really want to know. Trust me when I tell you, I was not a quick study on this fact. I intuitively knew I should never ask for justifications for the oddball things they pulled, but I couldn't help myself. With Lily, at least in the early years, I never did ask, not just because she didn't have the words to tell me, but because the answer was usually obvious.

But, clearly, Lily had her disconnects too, like sitting in a six-foot-wide play pool with two other children and expecting them not to splash. Lily took each drop that landed in her eye personally and let them know so with her ear-piercing screams. Then she cried when I made her get out of the pool. It wasn't so much Terry's and Jimmy's feelings I was trying to spare, but the neighbor's ear drums. It couldn't have been easy living next to us. We must have had a neighborhood full of saints because we never got one complaint. In fact, the neighbors to our north, came over in tears, a basketful of sandwiches in hand, the day the moving van came for mine and Lily's stuff.

The hard thing about the Parkinson's is it put an end to the life I had promised myself if I just soldiered through the years when the children were growing up. I had calculated that as soon as Lily turned 20, I could find a nice group home for her and pamper myself with a few of the finer things: A trip to New England to tour homes of Robert Frost, Nathaniel Hawthorne, Eugene O'Neill, Henry David Thoreau and Louisa May Alcott. A trip alone to the grocery store. A car that was made within the decade and comfortably seats only two. A new wood floor, preferably wormy chestnut. A cup of coffee enjoyed without interruption. A crisp white button-down-the-front shirt made of 100 percent cotton and a pair of linen trousers, which I never before had time to iron. A piece of family room furniture not upholstered in micro-fiber, set atop a vegetable-died oriental rug laid out without fear of play dough becoming encrusted into its Angora fibers. Although, I would have forfeited all of the above for one thing. I had plans to rescue my books from the boxes in the garage, knock down the wall between the children's rooms, build floor-to-ceiling knotty alder book shelves and furnish my library with a down-stuffed purple velvet wing-back chair positioned at a 45-degree angle to the northern window with a reading lamp showering full spectrum, high definition light over my parcel of private paradise. If I had enough money left, I'd get one of those rolling ladders only rich people with proper English own. Not that my ceilings were high enough to justify one, but it would have served as a symbol that no material thing was more important to me than my books. I could have graduated magna cum laude from the Anna Quindlen school of interior design. The author once said, "I would be the most content if my children grew up to be the kind of people who think decorating consists mostly of building enough bookshelves."

But here I am at the end of my life without a single bookcase. There's a small box on the closet floor that has a dozen of my favorite books. That is the extent of my library. Not that a library would do me any good at this point, since I am too shaky to read. But books are like old friends. It would be nice to be surrounded by them in my final days. At least I will leave a legacy when I go. I have passed on my love of books to Lily. When she was little I used to spend hours reading to her. Well, even when she wasn't so little. We'd huddle on the couch under a blanket on a rainy Sunday afternoon devouring the classics -- *Journey to the Center of the Earth, 20,000 Leagues Under the Sea, Sherlock Holmes*. She loved action and adventure and mystery -- tales that usually appeal to boys. You could skip *Pollyanna* and *Little Women* as far as she was concerned. She'd always tell me how much her Daddy was like the main character of whatever book we were reading. I think Lily probably has her father pegged as a brilliant professor, a submarine captain and case-cracking consulting detective all rolled into one. What man could ever live up to that? But, I know Lily. She's not looking for a hero. She would love him if he was nothing but a tree stump. As long as he is a kind and affectionate tree stump who will let her hug him and call him Daddy. As for me, I'd be OK with a tree stump, too. Actually, I would prefer it to all the other frightening possibilities.

12

THE DADDY

After four weeks, Lily has finally been released from the hospital. She is continuing to recover at home with the help of a visiting nurse. Now that Lily is out of the woods, my doctor has forbidden me to leave the Manor House. My blood pressure has been at an all-time low and all the symptoms of the Parkinson's have worsened. The days without Lily are unbearable. I am beginning to understand the hell everyone else here in this nursing home is living through. People on the outside seem to think we don't know we are lonely, that, like dogs waiting at the door for their master's to return, we don't feel the passage of time. They seem to think we forget how we are supposed to be treated, that we are not fully aware of our misery, that our failing memories and eyesight somehow dull our emotions. People equate the elderly with small children and in many ways it is true. We are just as helpless and vulnerable. Neither one of us has a voice, so it's easy to ignore our pain. Which explains the common practice of circumcising a newborn without general anesthesia. When the baby cries, we call it discomfort. It may very well be intolerable pain, but people have no way of remembering. We justify it by believing infants have a limited knowledge of their surroundings and that supposedly dulls the pain of the snip. For the elderly, their limited intellect must also dull their suffering. Wouldn't it follow? But all my life, I've never felt the kind of misery that I live with every day Lily can't come. The physical agony of Parkinson's doesn't even touch the anguish of loneliness. I'm not the only one who feels the void. I probably field the same question a hundred times a day. "How's Lily?" I never grow weary of answering. I want to talk about her. It somehow brings her closer when I do. The thought of her is the only reason my feet touch the floor in the morning. The thought of her coming back. "We're praying for her," people say, in the same upbeat tone that you would tell someone you're routing for their team. I had heard of prayer warriors before, but folks around here are more like Heaven's cheerleading squad. There is a confidence about them that, if I didn't know better, would make me think they know something that I don't. That there's only one possible outcome. That she is going to come strolling through that door any day now. Even Buddy, whose never been known to say a kind word to anyone wheeled past me one day and said, in a stale monotone, "I hope your daughter gets better real soon." He said it like a man who's been forced to make nice with someone he's holding a grudge against.

****

Agnes is in the lounge playing cards with her priest. He is a tall man in his mid-30s, with dark hair and a worn-down Texas accent. There were only hints of a twang left, on words like "much" and "time" and "holy."

"Hi ho, Bev," Agnes says, more cheerfully than usual. "You remember Father Fitz."

"Hello, Bev," he says, standing to shake my hand. "Would you like to join us in a game of hearts?"

"Oh, no thank you, Father," I say. "I'm feeling a bit under the weather."

My hands are so shaky, the cards would probably fly everywhere. I don't want someone I hardly know to witness that.

Father Fitz sits back down, and he and Agnes finish their game as I watch. Then the priest strikes the cards into a tidy stack.

"Would you like to walk outside in the garden for a bit, Beverly" he asks me.

"I'm not sure I can make it all the way out there," I say. I only like to go with Lily, who knows my gait well enough to diminish the odds of my falling.

"You can lean on me," he says, offering me his arm.

When we get to the garden, Father leads me to a white wicker chair under a shade tree, even though it is overcast.

"So, Bev," he says, "Agnes tells me you might need to talk."

"Talk?"

"Yes, she told me you had made reference to something you've been carrying around for a long time, but she didn't know what it was, and she thought maybe talking to a guy wearing a Roman collar might help." He smiles so large that a vein pops out near his left temple and I notice his crow's feet for the first time.

I smile back. "Good old Agnes. She is a true friend."

"That she is," he says, putting one foot across the opposite knee and grabbing his shin with both hands. "I can even hear a confession, if you would like."

"Well, that's nice of you. I'll have to come over some time. It's Queen of Peace parish, right?"

"Yes that's right," he says. "But we could do it right here, too."

"Here?" I say looking around. I don't know why I find that so odd. It's not as if we were at Kreielsheimer Promenade. He and I are the only ones outside. It looks like it is about to drizzle.

"I don't think I remember how to go to confession," I tell him. "The last time I went, I was a teenager on a confirmation retreat and I don't even know how many years ago that was, and I don't remember how to do the math."

"So, you just start like this," he says. "Bless me Father for I have sinned. It's been far too long since my last confession."

"Do I have to confess all my sins -- for my entire life?"

"All that you can remember at the moment," he says.

"You will be old and gray like me by the time I am through," I say.

He lets out a hearty laugh. "I've got nothing but time," he says. "And that's not even mine, but the Lord's."

All of a sudden, I feel a little trapped. But his warmth has charmed me. I can tell he is a genuinely good person. He has trustworthy eyes, safe to look into and lay bare your soul. Not because he is wearing a Roman collar and is bound by the seal of Confession, but because that's the kind of person he is. Whether he'd been a plumber or a priest, he would keep a secret safe and resist the temptation to form theories about what kind of person you are based on failings of your past. Still, I don't want to say the words I have locked up in the basement for so many years. I don't want to hear them out loud. I could go to my grave without ever hearing them.

Father Fitz is watching a couple of birds drink dew off the grass blades. As if that made him suddenly thirsty, he asks, "Would you like some coffee?" He stands and pokes his black shirt into his polyester trousers with his thumbs, stretching out his torso. "I could use a cup."

"Sure, OK," I say. "Thank you."

"Cream and sugar?"

"No thank you. Just black."

It takes him longer to return than I expected and I imagine he must have gotten caught in a conversation with someone inside. Maybe he's even absolving sins. He smiles as soon as he comes into view, carrying two Styrofoam cups. His smile remains as he hands me one and sits down.

"You know, there are certain things in our past that once we say them they don't seem so frightening anymore," he says, looking into his cup of black coffee and swirling it slightly. "Look at it this way. People pay $120 an hour for psychotherapy so they can talk about all those things they've got to get off their chest. My services: free." He winks as he holds the cup up, as if to toast his own cleverness before bringing it back down to his lips.

"Definitely a bargain," I say, smiling. We watch the wrens fly on and off the grass. I wonder what he is thinking during the long stretch of silence. I am thinking how nice it would be to be one of those birds and fly away -- not from Father Fitz, just from this place.

"It's like a cancer patient who doesn't want to take chemo because it makes them lose their hair," says Father. "Then, they are, one day, in great agony when it becomes apparent that they are going to die and they could have done something about it."

He takes a sip of his coffee, blinking at the heat of it.

"We're all a little bit like that, Bev. We all suffer from the cancer of sin. There is a cure, but we don't want to take the medicine because it costs us a bit of our pride. Confession is like chemo. You might lose your hair. But you will gain your life."

"It's just, you know, Father," I say, "and I'm sure Agnes must have told you. No disrespect to you or your Church, but I'm just not much of a believer."

"In confession?"

"In God."

"Well, faith is a gift, offered freely to all." He takes another sip. "I will pray for you to receive it."

"Thank you, Father." I am sincere about my thanks. I actually would like to believe in something, especially at this stage of my life. And if anyone could order up a miracle, it might be this man.

"In the meantime," he says, "you might as well make a good confession. What have you got to lose? If I'm right and there is a God, you'll be able to set things straight with Him. If I'm wrong, you'll still save yourself 120 bucks."

"I'll think about that, Father. But, in the meantime, do you mind if I ask you a philosophical question?"

"Not at all. But, just to warn you, I am not much of a philosopher."

"But you are a wise man, I can tell, and I seem to lack wisdom. I have been asking myself this question for thirty years and I can't figure out the answer." I look into the sky and notice a cloud shaped like a turtle. "Father, are all promises meant to be kept?"

He places his hand on the back of his head and smoothes out his thick hair, gazing down at the grass. "If time stood still, perhaps. But time changes things." He looks into the sky, at the turtle. "And yet, our words are the building blocks of our relationships. And if our words are eroded by the passage of time, how can our relationships stand?"

"So, you don't know the answer either," I smile.

He smiles back at me. "I know that God always keeps His promises. He is all-knowing, the Lord of all history, the Lord of the present moment and the Lord of what is to come. He is wise enough to know the promises he should be making. That's not always the case with us, and yet, we must always try to imitate God in His infinite love."

"So the answer is no."

"The answer is to do what love requires."

"How do you know what love requires?"

"I will pray that you are guided by the wisdom of the Holy Spirit." He grabs my hand and squeezes it until the warmth from his hand transfers to mine. "I am really enjoying our conversation, Bev," he says, glancing at his watch, "but unfortunately, we'll have to continue it another time. I'm scheduled to meet with a couple I'm going to marry."

"Oh, how nice," I say, trying not to look disappointed at his leaving.

"Would you like to go back inside?" he says, offering me his arm.

"No," I say, patting his wrist. "I'll stay here for a while and watch the birds."

"OK," he says smiling. He reaches into his shirt pocket and pulls out a card. "Here, take this, Bev, and call me if you need anything. And tell Agnes I said good-bye, and I'll be back to visit her soon. And you too."

"OK, Father. Thank you."

I watch him go in the door and through the lobby and wish I could say, "There goes my priest, my friend." I look down at his card. On the front it says, "Father John Fitzpatrick O.F.M.," his cell phone and the parish information. I flip the card over.

"All shall be for Him, all! And even when I have nothing to offer Him I will give Him that nothing. --Saint Therese of Lisieux"

St. Therese. Isn't that who Terry is named for? I let out a small chuckle at the suitability of the quote. I definitely had nothing to offer.

****

Greta Schenck, who runs the cafeteria, interviewed me last week about Lily's favorite foods. She has been preparing a handsome feast -- well, as handsome as food can be at a place that deposits mashed potatoes on your plate with an ice cream scooper. It's been seven weeks since the accident, and Lily is making her return to the Manor House. The staff has decorated with orange and fuchsia streamers and all the residents have signed a long computer-generated banner that says "Welcome Back, Lily. We Missed You!"

Agnes is playing lookout and tells us in a hushed voice the distinguished guest has arrived. A wave of welcoming voices rush at Lily through the automatic sliding doors and stop her in her tracks as if she'd just hit a wall. She stands stunned, mouth open, eyebrows up, looking around with quick jerks of her head.

"We all missed you so much, we wanted to throw you a party?" says Agnes.

"Welcome back, baby," I say grabbing her hand and bringing it to my lips. My hand is trembling so much, it knocks her knuckles against my mouth several times before I manage a kiss.

"A party?" She smiles wide and shakes her head in disbelief. Lily is baffled by all the attention. What was the big deal, returning from the brink of death?

"A party for you, Honey," I say. "We're so glad you're back."

The shock wears away enough for her to bend over and squeeze me hard. I wanted to cry, I had missed that hug so much.

She gives them out freely to patients and nurses alike. She is working the crowd. Buddy wheels over to her, and without moving any muscles in his face, except for possibly one in his bottom lip, he says, "I'm glad you're feeling better."

"Thank you," Lily says, throwing her arms around his neck. He stiffens up and then his arms slightly relax and bend awkwardly around her thick waist. Everyone surrounds them, throwing looks of bewilderment at each other. Then comes a unison of smiles and a collective gasp as she kisses him on the top of the head. He wheels off into his corner and silently watches the festivities like a character in a wax museum. Every now and then, Lily looks over and smiles at him and he responds with a slight nod.

It is going to be absolute torture watching her walk out that door this evening. And every evening after that. What if something happens to her again? It's like having an eight-year-old out there wandering around in the world alone.

I have asked Lily many times what happened the night of the accident. Did she not see the bus? Did she even look to see if anything was coming? Lily can't remember a thing. But she swears she always looks both ways. Left, then right and then left again. So where did that bus come from? She doesn't know.

"Lily, it's important you try to remember, so you'll know what happened and you won't make the same mistake again." I nag her once more -- after the party is over.

"I don't know, Mommy," she whines. "I try my best."

"I'm not blaming you, Honey," I say. "I just want you to be safe. I can't bear to think that could happen again."

"OK. I be more careful."

She says it as if I were asking her not to spill her juice again. Should I encourage her to make fewer visits? No, it would be pointless. She'd never listen to me. She loves coming here too much. But there is something else to consider too. Regardless of whether I decide to keep my promise to my sister, replacing me with another old person might not be the best solution. All the time Lily has spent with me is time she hasn't spent with people her own age. What interests has she cultivated outside this stagnant nursing home? I can't let her continue to invest all her time here, neglecting her own life. One time, many years ago, I read a comment on YouTube about how a teenager with Down Syndrome grieved when his grandparents died.

"Every night for 16 years, Benny had ice cream with his grandpa, then his grandma read him a story. Then one day, she died. That was 4 years ago. So then, every night Benny had ice cream with his grandpa, went into grandma's room, took down an article of her clothing, held it to his face, then sat quietly on her bed, waiting for his story, perhaps. Or listening. Now Grandpa is dying. Benny sits at the table and waits, his ice cream melting in front of him. Waiting for grandpa, who will never come. After a while he pushes the bowl away, untouched."

I have to try to help Lily deal with my death before I die.

"Lily, I think it's too dangerous for you to make the trip over here so much," I tell her. "I want you to cut your visits to twice a week."

"No, Mommy," she says, putting both fists on her chest. "It will hurt my heart on the days I don- see you."

"No, Honey," I say, trying to use my most reassuring voice, but realizing the Parkinson's has robbed me of virtually all my abilities to communicate with any kind of expression. "You can find fun things to do. You know, you could go out with your bowling league or go to a movie with Gwenny. You could maybe even go on a few dates. Go out to eat with some handsome fellow."

"But who feed you?" she asks. "And brush your hair?"

"The nurses," I say. "That's what they get paid for."

"But you said you don- like how they do it as much as me."

"Well, I don't," I say. "No one can do things like my Lily. But I want you to go out and have some fun."

"No," she says, shaking her head. "I wanna be with you."

"But, darling. You're spending all your time here." I reach out for her hand and she places hers in mine. "You know that I'm not going to be here forever, right?"

"Wha- you mean?"

I wish she would make this easier for me.

"Well, I'm not really well, you know," I say, "and people don't, you know, stay here forever."

"You mean go to Heaven?"

"Yes."

"Like my first Mommy."

"Yes."

I watch her face for a while. She is looking down at our clasped hands. One foot is folded under the opposite thigh and she is swinging the dangling foot back and forth under the chair. The sight of her eyelashes can still make me want to cry. Finally she looks up into my eyes.

"Wha- you gonna do when you see her?" she asks.

"Your Mommy?"

"Umm-hmmm."

"I'm going to give her a big hug," I say. "No, two big hugs. One from me and one from you."

"Do you think God let me come with you?" Lily asks.

"You have a big, long life to live here first," I pat her on the leg. "You're going to do great things."

"Wha- great things can I do?" she asks.

"Well, for starters, you're the only person in the entire world who can be Lily. The world needs a Lily very badly."

"Wha- about Heaven?" she says.

"What about it, Baby?"

"Heaven need a Lily? I can do great things there, too."

This is definitely a conversation I have no credentials for. I'm not even sure there is a Heaven. Now I have to answer deep theological questions worthy of papal encyclicals.

"I think if Heaven needed you more than earth needed you," I reason, "you wouldn't have survived that bus accident."

"Are you excited?

"For what?" I ask.

"To go to Heaven?"

I shake my head. "No," I say. "I'd rather stay here with you."

She looks puzzled and a bit skeptical and then smiles.

"Now," I say, bringing my face in closer to hers. "What two days a week would you like to come visit me?"

I learned early on that it was best to give Lily choices within boundaries. She is always more compliant that way.

"All of them," she says with no hint of irony.

"But, remember, we just talked about picking only two days a week. Do you want to come Sunday and Wednesday?"

"No. Tuesday bingo night."

"OK, how about Tuesdays and Saturdays."

"No, Mass."

"OK. Tuesdays and Sundays."

"Nope. Wednesday meat loaf."

"Well, you're going to have to give up something, Lily," I say, almost beat down by the classic Lily stubbornness. "But you'll find something else even better to do on those nights that you don't come here. Now, pick two days."

"I can't," she says. "My heart will hurt."

"OK. See, look," I say. "Today's Monday, right? So why don't you not come tomorrow and Wednesday and come Thursday. And when you come Thursday, I want to hear all about what you did on Tuesday and Wednesday. We'll have so many interesting things to talk about."

She is looking down at her hands, silently.

"OK, Lily?"

"OK."

I put my hand under her chin and lift. Her chin catches a slight tremor from my shaking hand. "I'll make a call to Mr. Fox and see if he can drive you and Gwenny to the club," I say. "You haven't gone out dancing in a long time, have you?"

"No."

"Does that sound like fun, then?"

"Uh-huh."

"OK, then. Will you do me a favor?"

"Uh-huh."

"Will you dance the *Macarena* for me. That's what I used to dance to when I was your age. Do you think they still play that one?"

"The *Ma-arena*?" She snickered. "I don- tink so, Mommy."

"How about *I Like to Move It*?

She shook her head and grinned.

Well, what's your favorite dance tune?" I ask her.

"S*taying Alive*."

Very appropriate for a young woman who has just survived a wrestling match with a city bus. I can't believe disco has made a comeback for a third time. I thought it was bad enough the first time around.

"Mommy?" she says. "Maybe I stay away for a while, and you not tired to see me anymore, I come back every day."

"Oh, Baby, I could never get tired of seeing you," I say. "I'm going to miss you something awful. But I want you to have a good life. There is so much more out there that is better than this place. Why don't you want to go?"

"Well, Heaven better than here and *you* don- wanna go."

Touché', Lily.

I ask if she wants to play a game and she waddles over to the cabinet to get the Dora the Explorer Memory game. Even when she was just six, she could beat me occasionally. Lily places the cards face down in very precise rows, but stops half-way into the third one.

"Where's Daddy?" she asks. "The Daddy with the puppy."

She must be remembering the baby picture taken when her father brought his puppy to visit. The photo was of Lily and the puppy. Her father wasn't even in the picture. But somehow Lily has never forgotten whatever she thinks she knows about him.

"Did Terry show you that picture while you were in the hospital?" I ask.

"Yeah," she says. "Daddy bring a puppy to play with me."

"Yes, that's right."

"I wan- him," she says.

"The puppy?"

"No, the Daddy."

"Finish laying out the cards, Lily," I say.

"Terry will find him," Lily says.

"No, Love. I don't think so. Terry doesn't know where he is."

"Terry promise. She look for him."

"Oh, I don't think she would have promised that, Lily," I say. "I think you probably misunderstood her. We don't even know his name."

"His name is Daddy. Terry look for him. She promise."

When Lily leaves the Manor House that evening, I kiss her and tell her I'll see her Thursday. But the next day comes and so does Lily. And the next. For a week, I gently remind her that she isn't supposed to be here. She says sorry and promises she'll try to remember not to visit the next day. The following Saturday, I feel safe that she won't show up because I set up a dinner with her and Gwenny. Lily calls once before the meal comes and once at dessert. She wants to tell me she has ordered my favorite -- cherry pie -- and did I want her to bring me a piece. I wish I could say I would still enjoy it. But that part of my life has passed and will never return. Eating is now a chore, necessary to sustain life. I long ago lost my appetite for cheesecake and mashed potatoes, or anything that has a consistency which lays heavy at the back of the mouth while waiting to be swallowed. I would have to make several false starts at getting it to go down before it finally went, and by then the adrenalin had reached my hands and caused needles to go through them for fear of choking. For some reason, I had always had trouble swallowing that kind of stuff anyway, ever since I was in seventh grade and they made us sit through a movie in gym class on how to perform the Heimlich maneuver.

On every day I don't set something up for her, Lily ends up here. I can't continue to be her cruise director forever. I am running out of ideas. And I fear people will run out of patience if I badger them too much about doing stuff with Lily. I am just going to have to give up trying to make her get a life outside this place and concede that this place is her life. At least for the time being. Soon enough, there will be nothing here for her and she will be forced to move on. If I have done my job well, she will. It just would have made me feel more at peace to see her settle into a new way of life before I go, so I would know what's going to happen to her. Although, my sister never had that luxury, and things turned out fine after all. I think Jen would be very happy to see us now, me and Lily. And if it makes Lily happy to be with me, I'm not going to deprive her of a single minute of it. There aren't that many minutes left. Anyway, there is still the remote possibility that Terry's freelance sleuthing might prove fruitful in filling the void left in Lily's life by my passing. If nothing else, Terry's promise puts an end to a lifetime of laboring over what to do with mine. And for that, I am grateful.

****

On Sunday evening, Terry calls. She wants to know if Lily has left yet, and I tell her she just did.

"Auntie Bev, I did a little research," Terry says.

"And you found Lily's father."

"Did Lily tell you I said I'd look for him?" Her voice is a bit strained now.

"Yes," I say. This conversation was beginning to remind me of all those we had when she was a teenager. She always got caught. At least I hope so. "She said you promised."

"Well, I didn't exactly promise," Terry says. "Lily started asking questions about that picture of her and the puppy."

"Well, now she really wants to see her father," I say. "I wish you hadn't brought it all up. We don't even know the man's name."

"Pablo Perez."

"What? How do you know that?"

"I got in touch with Mom's best friend -- the lady who used to work with her. She told me his name."

"Calli Flannery?"

"Yeah."

"I remember her," I say. I try to remember why I had lost contact with her. I so enjoyed her writing and the stories she would tell me about Jen.

"Terry, as curious as we may be, I don't think we should go against your mother's wishes. She asked me never to contact him."

"She did? When? That doesn't sound like Mom. She pretty much lived her life like an open book."

"Well, this chapter was closed," I say.

"Well, it's open now," Terry says. "I have his phone number."

"He's still alive."

"He's only 62."

"You must have the wrong person, Honey," I say. "He's got to be older than that. Do the math."

"It's the right person, Auntie."

"How can you be so sure?" I ask. "There's got to be oodles of Pablo Perezes."

"I called him."

"What? Why didn't you tell me you were going to do this, Terry?"

"What's the big deal?" she says. "He was glad to hear about Lily. That she was doing well and everything."

"The big deal is it's strictly against your mother's wishes," I say.

"Mom told you that if Lily ever wants to track down her father, she should be forbidden?"

"No, but--." I almost slipped and told her I had once tried to find another home for Lily. "She never would elaborate, Terry. But she told me not to contact him back when she was sick. She must have had a good reason. I made a promise."

"She couldn't have meant *never* contact him," Terry says. "Anyway, *I* didn't promise. You did."

"Well, I hope you didn't invite him to Thanksgiving Dinner," I say. "You know nothing about this man."

"He seems like a very nice man, Auntie," Terry says. "Real salt of the earth. Gentle and soft-spoken."

"You got all of this from a telephone conversation?" I say. "Your mother knew him quite a bit better than that, and she didn't want anything to do with him, for some reason."

She is silent for several seconds and finally says, "Well, people change. They grow up. He's an elderly school custodian. How much of a menace to society could he be?"

"He could be a pedophile," I say. "And he's not that elderly."

Speaking of which, I still needed to do the math. Jen would be 76 now if she were alive. That makes him 14 years younger than her. That means she was 39 and he was 25. Oh my.

Terry told me she had to hang up and go settle a dispute between her children and she would call me soon.

"Wait, hold on," I tell her. "At least tell me what you plan to do next? Did you tell him you would put him in touch with Lily or anything?"

"He said he'd like to talk with her on the phone."

"When?"

"I don't know. I gave him her phone number at the group home." I can hear in the background the children have turned up the volume on their disagreement. "I really have to go, Auntie, before someone kills someone here. I'll keep you posted if I hear anything, and you do the same for me."

"OK," I say. "Kiss the kids for me."

"Kisses back to you Auntie," Terry says.

"Oh, Terry," I say, "I won't mention anything to Lily. In case he doesn't call."

I hang up and sit silent for a while, doing nothing. I keep trying to imagine how my sister got involved with a man that much younger than she was. And why did she sever contact with him? Or him with her? They did, after all, have a child together. You'd think that would warrant at least an occasional post card. Something comes bubbling up in my esophagus. It is either the Salisbury steak or the anxiety of opening the door to whatever it was that made my sister slam it shut. I ring for the nurse to bring me a Rolaids.

13

CHEMO

Not everyone around here gets a memorial, but Father Fitz is holding one for Agnes in the chapel today after daily Mass. Agnes' children have flown her body home to Wisconsin. She died in her sleep early Sunday morning. Heart attack. I still can't believe she's gone. I don't know why I always assumed I would die before her, even though she was five years older. I never considered that I might be in this place without her.

The memorial is simple. Father Fitz says some prayers and talks about how he was told by all the deacons that she sat in the front row of that chapel every day. He tells how he first came to the Manor House because he was filling in for a deacon who was sick and couldn't make it out to preside over the Communion service.

"After Mass that day," Father tells the small gathering of patients and nurses, "this tiny lady, wearing a white shawl that reminded me of sheep's fleece, wheeled herself up to me and pressed a prayer card of St. Therese in my hand and said she was going to offer all her sufferings for my priesthood. On the prayer card was this quote from St. Therese: "

'All shall be for Him, all! And even when I have nothing to offer Him I will give Him that nothing.'"

Father Fitz says, on that day, his destiny changed. He had gone into seminary with great hopes of someday being a bishop,

145

or who knows, maybe even a cardinal. After he met Agnes, he no longer saw the priesthood as a career, but as a calling to win souls for God, one at a time in quiet humility. He became a devotee to the cloistered Carmelite nun, who had lived her life in obscurity.

Lily got the morning off from work to attend the memorial. She wept so hard when I told her Agnes had passed away, it scares me to think about how she will suffer when I die. They say adolescents and adults with Down Syndrome are at a higher risk for depression than other people, especially after someone dies. I believe that's because they feel so deeply. The bigger the love, the more profound the loss. Like a child, Lily is pure, raw, unedited emotion. I ache for what lies in her future and wish she could form a deep attachment to another human being before I go. Thanks to Terry, there might be a chance of that.

When Father Fitz asks the rest of us to share memories of Agnes, Lily is the first to raise her hand. Father smiles at her and motions her to the lectern. As she stands, talking into the microphone, I think back to when she was a little girl of 5 or 6 and couldn't say more than 20 words, most of which were unintelligible. I never would have believed back then that I would be hearing that child give a public address. But there she is telling about how Agnes always had a smile for her and gave her a blessing as she left every night.

"She was a real nice lady," she says. I'm not sure how many people understand what she is saying, given her speech impediment, sinuses full of tears and a mouth far too close to the microphone, but there wasn't a dry eye in the room just the same. "She always made my heart happy," she says of Agnes. "I love her. And I can't wait to see her in Heaven."

If there is a Heaven, Agnes and Lily are well-fit for it. And then there is me. I don't know if it is the grief of losing Agnes or the anxiety of almost losing Lily, but the thought of never seeing the two of them again -- or Terry or Jimmy -- suddenly becomes too much to bear. I am in anguish, sunk deep into a bottomless loss with no way up. And not just a loss of Agnes, but a loss of every other person I've ever loved, because one day, most likely one day in the next year, I will no longer be here. So I sit here and wonder, if there is a God, will I get points for raising Lily? Could agreeing to lay down my life for her get me into Heaven? Or would I have so many penalties for yelling at her that it will be a wash?

Lily returns to her seat, and I give her a tissue from one of the many Kleenex boxes somebody has placed on the seats throughout the small chapel. She blows her nose loud.

When it is my turn to talk about Agnes, I recount the tale of how she befriended me. I was quite depressed at having just lost my home and the privilege of living with my daughter. I had decided I wasn't ever going to come out of my room. So, the second day I was here, I hear this little knock on the door. It was Agnes, coming by to welcome me. She told me she had come about two weeks prior and that the place was shaping up to be exactly the hell-hole she had imagined. She had a remedy, she said, but I would have to follow her to her room. I told her I'd have to take a rain check because I was just so beat from the move.

"What did you bring with you," she asked, "if you don't mind my being nosey."

Well, I didn't mind, but I thought it was odd. I told her I'd brought some shirts and slacks, some lipstick and blush, a hair dryer and brush and a box of books."

"What kind of books?" she asked.

"Over there in the corner," I motioned, "if you'd like to look through them."

I had brought them with me more for the sight and the feel of them than I did for the words inside because I couldn't do much reading anymore and they were above Lily's reading level.

"Oh, I love Dickens," Agnes said peering down into the box. "Have you read Oliver Twist?"

We talked a bit about favorite authors. I was tempted to tell her she could borrow some books, but I was afraid I'd never see them again. They were the last remnants of my vast library, which Terry and Jimmy divided between them and, I'm sure, immediately stowed in their respective attics, sealing the fate of their pages to jaundice by neglect and humidity.

Agnes asked what my last name was. When I told her she said, "Oh, as in Horace Greeley, the newspaper man who said 'Go West, young man.'"

Dang, I thought. This woman is sharp as tacks. How old is she?

I asked her last name and when she told me I said, "Oh, as in billionaire Leonardo Del Vecchio, the eyewear magnate."

Agnes looked at me like I was nuts and then chuckled. "Now how on earth do you know that?"

"I read -- well, used to read -- Forbes."

"And..."

"Well, his name stuck in my head because his mother sent him away to an orphanage when he was seven because she couldn't afford five children. So I just always wondered what that must be like for a mother, who was so desperately poor, to have the son she gave up become a billionaire. I mean, did he resolve right then and there, the day she left him at the orphanage, never to be poor because it's just too darned painful?"

Agnes shook her head and looked half disgusted and half amazed. "Del Vecchio is my husband's name. I don't think there's any relation to Leonardo. My Joey's family is from Italy, though -- Naples."

"Did you ever go?"

"Oh, yes," she said. "Plenty."

"I've always wanted to go," I said.

"Uh-huh, nice place," Agnes nodded. "But I never understood the Italians. The first thing they say when they see you is how fat you've gotten. The second thing they tell you is to sit down and eat. Speaking of which, Beverly, I've got to run and get ready for dinner."

She impressed upon me the necessity to come visit her. Room 122, second from the end of the hall.

"I'll see you in the dining room in a few minutes," she said cheerfully as she wheeled herself out. I didn't tell her I had directed staff to bring me my meals in bed. The next day she showed up around 2 in the afternoon at my door, with a large wooden box on her lap. It was a smooth mahogany with a fancy brass clasp.

"Well," she said, "since you didn't come to my place, I had to bring a little piece of sanity to yours." She opened the box to reveal the largest selection of tea bags I have ever seen. There must have been three dozen different varieties. The way they were arranged in the box was artistic -- linear, symmetrical and colorful, like a piece of modern art you'd see hanging over an armless black leather couch imported from Copenhagen. She reached behind her, unhooked the bag hanging to her wheelchair and set my rolling bed table with a small electric tea kettle, two crimson Fiestaware mugs and a bag of Walkers Scottish shortbread. "High tea," she said smiling. "I figure we could read a little and sip a little and read a little more."

I told her I couldn't read very well because of the Parkinson's. It would be like trying to read during an earthquake. That was one of my biggest sorrows.

"Lily tries to help me out by reading to me sometimes," I said. "But she has Down Syndrome, so Magic Tree House is about as lofty as it gets. I've heard the whole series. They were quite popular when my kids were growing up."

"Oh yes, I remember well," Agnes said. She told me she'd be happy to read to me in the afternoons while we had our tea. I never did have the heart to tell her that, since I have no sense of taste, I couldn't tell an Oolong from an Earl Grey. Or from a piping hot cup of steeped gym socks, for that matter.

Agnes was so deeply good. It would be obvious to anyone why someone would befriend her. But I didn't. It was the other way around. To this day, I don't know why she singled me out as her best friend.

After the memorial I see Father Fitz out the windows of the double French doors. He is in the garden with his head down, elbows resting on his knees, rosary dangling from his clasped hands. I wonder if this is the last time I will see him, since he came mainly to see Agnes. I make my way out to him.

"Father?"

He looks up from his Rosary.

"I'm ready to lose my hair," I say.

A smile creeps across his face. "Praise God."

He stands up, puts an arm around me and eases me onto the bench. He sits beside me, makes the sign of the cross and says a short prayer I've never heard before and don't remember now.

"Bless me, Father, for I have sinned," I say, my faint voice shaking in rhythm with my hands. "It's been 62 years since my last confession."

14

ESTUPIDEZ OF YOUTH

I haven't been outside since the day I was absolved. The November chill is setting in and it's not so pleasant to be out anymore. I can't help but wonder if I'll ever see that garden again. I wouldn't bet that I will live to see spring.

But the last thing I need to add to all my shaking is a shiver. The bursts of cold that come through the automatic doors of the lobby are all the fresh air I can tolerate right now. Lily brings quite a large gust with her as she bounds through the sliding doors and swoops in on my neck with her enthusiastic embrace.

"Mommy, Mommy," she's trying to catch her breath. "You have any money I can have?"

"What for, Baby?" I say, trying to loosen her grip on my neck, so I can see into her eyes.

"I go on a trip to see Daddy."

"Daddy"

"The Daddy with the puppy."

"Oh," I say, gripping both her hands to pull myself to a standing position. "Did you talk to him?"

"Yeah," she smiles wide. She puts her feet on auto-pilot, walking backwards in front of me at an intuitively perfect pace for my decrepit legs. "He call me on the phone."

"Is he nice?" I ask.

Yeah. Very nice," she says. "Can I go on a bus to see him?" We're halfway down the hall and I'm not sure I'm going to make it all the way to my room.

"Hmmm," I say. "I don't know. That's a long way. What did you two talk about on the phone."

"Stuff," she says.

"Stuff?"

"Lots of stuff."

"Did he invite you to come see him?"

"No," she says. "I gonna surprise him. From the bus stop." She is so excited, she is squeezing my hands, almost to the point of pain.

"Well, I don't have any money to give you for a bus trip right now, Lily," I say. "And even if I did, that's a very long way for you to travel alone, don't you think? Maybe he can come and visit you sometime."

"No," she says. "He got no money."

"He said that?"

"Yeah," she says, easing me on to my bed. "What's a janitor?"

"Someone who cleans up," I say. "Can you put my feet up on the bed, Love?"

"That sounds wonderful," she says, as if I had just told her a janitor was a kind of rock star. "He clean up at my other Mommy's newspaper."

"I thought he cleaned up at a school."

"He say he clean up and Mommy write stories."

All of a sudden, it all made sense. The book proposal Jen had written, like all good fiction, was based on a true story. She had fallen in love with the janitor of the *Burbank Register*.

"Lily, Honey, would you mind getting me some ice water?" I hand her Agnes' crimson Fiestaware mug, left in my room after the last cup of tea we had together. Lily loves the noisy ice machine in the hallway outside the dining room.

"Sure Mommy," she says.

"Then we'll play a game of Clue, OK?" I say.

Agnes' absence means that the essence of my existence has been reduced to the four hours between Lily's arrival and the end of visiting hours. That is literally the only thing I live for. All day, I watch the clock between TV game shows and an occasional Bingo game.

The Parkinson's has left my voice faint, which has contributed to a considerable amount of loneliness around here, where no one seems to hear you unless you're speaking through a bullhorn. Lily's a bit hard of hearing, but she's always so close to me (she'd spend the day in my lap if I'd let her) she doesn't have much trouble understanding me. I wish I could say the same were true for me as she was growing up.

While Jimmy and Terry were young, I never let them say that something didn't make sense. Physics makes sense. Algebra makes sense. Traffic laws make sense. It's just that you don't understand them. One day, in my frustration to try to figure out Lily, I told her she never made any sense. "Yes, she does, Auntie Bev," Terry argued, "You just don't understand her." It was true.

For months, I tried to figure out why Lily would ask for orange juice and then yell at me for giving it to her. Then one day she finally did the sign for "more" instead of screaming. "More?" I said. "I gave you some already and you haven't drank it." Back to screaming at me. This conversation played itself out four times a day for another year until one day I bent down to look into her face and explain it yet one more time. As I glanced over at the cup, from her angle, I finally saw what she had been so upset over for so long. Peering through the semi-transparent pink plastic, you could see the cup was only two-thirds full, not filled to the top as it appeared when you looked down on it. The way the cup was shaped, larger at the top than the bottom, it meant Lily was getting cheated out of quite a bit of liquid refreshment. From that day forward, I filled the cup to the top, expecting to have to mop up a few spills, but figuring it would be worth it to save my ear drums. Do you know, I can't remember her ever spilling a drop. Which is more than I can say for myself.

"Not too full, OK, Love," I tell Lily as she walks to the door to go get my ice water, though I know she won't listen. Even to this day, she always makes sure anything in a cup comes right to the top. "My hands are shaking like crazy tonight and I don't want to spill it."

****

It's mid-morning and a *Monk* rerun is playing in the lounge, but I can't follow the plot line. I'm trying to imagine scenarios for the estrangement between my sister and the janitor. I can understand an unintended drifting apart over the years, but that isn't the sort of thing that would require Jen to emphatically dissuade any contact with him. It wasn't an ideal situation, was what she said. What did that mean? If it were anyone but Jen, I would have chalked it up to a class thing. What professional would want to admit they had an affair with someone who sweeps floors for a living? But Jen was exactly the kind of person who would. She did not see herself any better than anyone else. Not even me.

I am glad Lily might finally have a father, especially since she will soon be orphaned again. But I want to talk to Pablo Perez myself, to make sure he isn't some nut case. And to tell you the truth, I really want answers to the mystery of my sister's past. I want to feel a renewed closeness to her. To learn something new about her would be to acquire more of her. This is why, I believe, people share their memories at funerals. It enlarges the space that lost person takes up in your insides, like a rediscovered long-lost episode makes a film vault all the more cherished. As the days go on, I become increasingly desperate to recover this pivotal episode that ushered new life into my sister's and destined me to live out the remainder of my days as the reluctant understudy to my sister's role. But most of all, I have to know why she and this man parted ways. This will provide the answer to why I have Lily and he does not. I got Pablo Perez's phone number from Terry last week. Every day I want to pick up the phone. I just don't know how to start the conversation with the father of my child, a man whom I have never met. I wish Agnes were here. Oh heck. I'm far too old to make procrastination practical. I dial.

"Bueno."

"Mr. Perez?"

"Yes?"

"I'm Beverly Greeley. Lily's Mom, uh, aunt. Jennifer Eagan's sister.

"Oh, yes, hello" he says. "Lily told me many beautiful things about you." He alliterated his T's like only people whose second language is English do.

"And you too," I say.

"Ah, thank you," he says. Terry was right. He is gracious and warm, and already I can see why Lily wants to step inside his life. I myself wish I could curl up on his couch with the Sunday comics and a cup of cocoa. I picture a small adobe-style home decorated with turquoise, orange and yellows and lots of inexpensive, yet meaningful art on the walls including a picture of Our Lady of Guadalupe.

"I just wanted to call and introduce myself."

"Wonderful," he says. "I'm so glad you did."

I am not sure how this conversation is going to wind its way around through the small talk to arrive at the reason for my call. I am going to have to help it along.

"Mr. Perez, I am old and ill, and I don't have much time left," I say, "and there are just some things I've always wondered. I hope you won't mind if I ask you, but if you do, please, just tell me it's too personal and I--"

"Please, Mrs. Greeley," he interrupts. "It's OK. I am an old man too, and I have long ago put pride aside. What would you like to know?"

How could my sister ever have let this one get away?

"I just have always wondered," I say. "What happened be-tween you and Jen."

"Well, of course, the most important thing that happened was Lily," he says.

"Yes, of course," I say. "But, how did it end? I mean, *why* did it end?"

He drew a long breath and released it slowly and unevenly.

"I'm sorry, Mr. Perez," I say, "if that question is too person-al--"

"No, no, no," he says, quick and rhythmic. "That is a ques-tion I have asked myself many times. And the only answer that I have come up with is estupidez -- stupid -- how you say? -- stu-pidity. The stupidity of youth."

"How so?" I say because there is a long pause and I want him to go on.

"When we found out Jen was expecting a baby, it became very scary -- for her and for me. We worked together, but we were from two different worlds. You know, many people would have not understood our love."

I felt a wave of warmth flush through me when he said "love."

"She was a very successful reporter, and I just mopped floors. Not even legally. I had a fake ID so I could work. I was sending every penny I could back to Mexico, so my family could have a tortilla and a bowl of broth to eat each day. And times were very difficult in America back then, Mrs. Greeley. I don't know if you remember. But Mexican immigrants were not very popular. Many people came to see us as a very large burden on the miserable economy."

A nurse pops her head in the door and notices I am on the phone. She squeezes her upper arm as a sign she wants to take my blood pressure. I nod my head and motion her in.

"Yes, I remember, Mr. Perez," I say, rolling up my pajama sleeve.

"Jen understood us like no one else. She had covered our community. She knew us. We were not just numbers to her. We were people with real lives, real families, real hunger." The blood pressure cuff squeezes hard. "And a real desire to live the American dream. I loved your sister, Mrs. Greeley. When she told me she was pregnant, it was OK with me. I had already seen my children in her eyes. I asked her to marry me. She said she would think about it."

The cuff deflates and my artery produces the obligatory throbs that make all medical personnel shake their heads, reach for their pens and scratch frantic notes onto my chart.

"Jen never wanted anyone at work to know whose baby she was having," Pablo Perez continues. "She said it was because of the policy of the company. We were not supposed to get romantically involved with coworkers. She said we had to keep our relationship quiet to protect our jobs, especially mine, she said, because I was already not very popular because of my heritage. Weeks went by and she never answered my marriage proposal. I assumed she didn't love me. She would tell me all the time she was too old and I was too pretty -- that's what she would call me." He let out a slight chuckle. "And she told me she was afraid that one day, when her days of youth were far behind her, mine would still be ahead. I thought she was trying to save my feelings, because I had no money. Then, one day she told me the baby had a disability. She assumed I would call off my proposal, but I did not. Still, she told me, she wanted to think about it. I don't mean to sound vain, Mrs. Greeley but when I was a young man, women found me very attractive. Many woman would -- how would you say -- hit on me. One day, a young woman did and I did not resist. Jen found out and it was over. She was not the kind of woman you could cheat on, Mrs. Greeley."

"That is certainly true," I say.

"But she assumed I started up a romance with someone else because the baby had Down Syndrome."

"And did you?" I ask, shocked at my own brashness. There is a long silence. "I'm sorry, Mr. Perez," I say. "For prying."

157

"Maybe I did, Mrs. Greeley," he says. His voice is tinged with sadness. "I don't know. Maybe I did."

I want to say something to let him know I completely understand. I get it. More than he will ever know. But anything I could say only sounds like wound dressings on a sore much too deep for gauze and white adhesive tape. It's best to just move forward.

"Are you planning to try to see Lily?" I ask.

"Yes, I would like to," he says.

"I know she would like that," I say.

"Do you think she could learn to accept me as her father?" He clears his throat. "I mean, over time."

"I think she has already done that, Mr. Perez."

"You know, I always wanted to see her," he says. "As she was growing up. Jen didn't want that."

"I know," I say. "She told me."

"She could never forgive me. She thought I was a two-timer, but she was wrong."

I know that's what they all say, but he has me convinced.

"I never fell in love again, Mrs. Greeley." His voice cracks a little. "Not like that."

I wonder what it would feel like to be loved like that.

"And without Lily, it's like a piece of me has always been missing," he continues. "I have always kept her picture in my wallet. I took it on her first birthday. That was the last time I ever saw her. It's the way Jen wanted it. She didn't want to keep seeing me."

"The hallmark of a true Eagan," I say. "Hard headedness. We were all blessed with it, I'm afraid, Mr. Perez."

He lets out a chuckle. "Lily too?"

"Like mother, like daughter."

"Uh-oh." There is joviality in his voice.

"But your life will be rich, Mr. Perez," I say. "With Lily in it."

"I have no doubt of that, Mrs. Greeley. None at all."

158

I sigh so heavily into the phone, I hear my breath rush back at me through the ear piece.

"Do you think she could --" Pablo Perez pauses to clear his throat again. "Do you think she could love me, Mrs. Greeley?"

I could tell it was a difficult question to ask, but it is easy to answer.

"Well, she loves *me,*" I say. "For some unfathomable and glorious reason, Mr. Perez. She loves me."

****

Father Fitz comes by every couple of weeks. It seems he is coming specifically to see me. Maybe as a tribute to Agnes. He knows she would be happy to see him treat me like something other than the lost cause that I am. As he makes his way down the hall to leave, he takes his thumb and draws invisible crosses on the foreheads of the patients he passes. He does it in such a tender way, for a split second, I see Agnes. It occurs to me that Father Fitz is what he is largely because of Agnes. Small, bent, discarded Agnes -- either by the power of prayer or power of suggestion -- changed that man's life and every person that comes in contact with him from now until he dies. He might already have changed mine, assuming it's not too late to believe in such things.

I wish I could be like Agnes. But I have bragging rights of my own -- a legacy fashioned from the remnants of my sister's life. What could I have said for the meaning of my life if it hadn't been for Lily? And Jimmy and Terry? Some nurse would have found my dead body in bed, and in packing up my belongings, she would have located an expired passport, an obsolete Blockbuster Rewards card and an old library volunteer photo ID. And she would have said to herself, "This was the essence of this woman's life." As it turns out, I have children to bury me, and they will speak for my essence. They will speak both with and without words.

I tell all this to you, my dear, beautiful Georgia -- the woman who has made my Jimmy so exceedingly happy -- because I want you to know what it is like to be the mother of a child with Down Syndrome. I give it to you honestly, unwrapped and without sugar coating. It's a difficult world to glimpse. But it is the world you will be thrust into if you decide to proceed with your pregnancy. I want you to know exactly what choice you are making -- what you are giving up if you decide to bring this child into the world. And what you are giving up if you decide not to. I'm not going to tell you what I would do in your situation. I'm sure you've got plenty enough people doing that. I'm just presenting you with the facts as clearly as I remember them.

I hope you know how much I love you and Jimmy and Terry and Jake and all the kids. You have all made me so very proud -- the lives you have chosen, the kind way that you treat people. My life is coming to an end soon, and I find myself wondering what's next. Jen never did send me any postcards, so I'm assuming she's having too much fun to stop and write. I'd like to think Heaven has a spot for someone like me and that angels will be there to greet me. One thing I know for certain. It will be Lily's face I long to see before I close my eyes for the last time. And if that final wish comes true, at least I'll have an angel to see me off.

About the Author

Sherry Boas began her writing career in a hammock in a backyard woods in rural Massachusetts when she was eight years old, writing a "novel" about the crime-fighting abilities of her Cocker Spaniel. Fourteen years later, she would draw her first writer's paycheck for a very different kind of story when she landed a job at a newspaper in Arizona. She spent the next decade as a journalist, winning news awards, but her heart still belonged to fiction. So, after twelve years at home with her four adopted and highly inspiring children, the words to *Until Lily* found themselves onto these pages. It is the first in a trilogy. The second and third sequels are *Wherever Lily Goes* and *Life Entwined with Lily's,* also available from Caritas Press. Visit www.lilytrilogy.com.